A Divine Christmas Ghost Story

Printed in the United States of America.
ISBN: 978-1-63385-432-1
Library of Congress Control Number: 2021914927

Illustration by: Teresa Emeloff
Additional Illustrations by: R. Caldecott

Layout and Design by Jason Price

Published by:
Word Association Publishers
205 Fifth Avenue
Tarentum, Pennsylvania 15084

www.wordassociation.com
1.800.827.7903

A Divine Christmas Ghost Story

Robert Cameron Malcolm IV

Acknowledgements and Dedication

special thank you goes out to Teresa Emeloff, a Highlands School District art teacher, for her marvelous illustrations featured on the first page of each chapter.

This book was a joy to write. Through the composition of this short story, I learned much about writing a novella. I am indebted to my former roommate at Westminster College, New Wilmington, Pennsylvania, Mr. Jeffrey Andrew Yeager for his help with this story. Jeff not only provided critical review of this work, but he also made helpful suggestions to improve the tale. He also performed the task of editing. His help was much appreciated. Without him, this book would not be as delightful as it is.

I am indebted to my wife, Laurie Ann Wright Malcolm who also critically reviewed the book, forwarded suggestions to me, and helped me with the editing.

Furthermore, I appreciate the help I received from The Reverend Jeffrey Scott Wylie, Rector of Christ's Church (ACNA) in Greensburg, Pennsylvania. Father Wylie, who was once a member of Natrona Heights Presbyterian

Church, assisted me by explaining Anglican nomenclature and practices.

Also assisting me with Anglican nomenclature was Father John Bailey of Christ Our Hope Anglican Church (ACNA) in Natrona Heights, Pennsylvania. Father Bailey served as one of my counselors at the Sports Camp I directed in the late 1980's and early 1990's. John's work at Pine Springs Presbyterian Camp in Jennerstown, Pennsylvania, in 1987 was most insightful and much appreciated.

It must also be noted that I had the Gothic and Cincinnati style of Natrona Heights Presbyterian Church much in mind as I wrote this story. This author had many experiences during his 30-year pastorate at that church. Some of these experiences are recorded in this book. Not everything in this book is fictitious.

Also mentioned in this book is St. Alban's Anglican Church in Murrysville, Pennsylvania. This church was the final church home of my cousins, W. Ross and K. Patricia Cogley Jones who lived in Delmont.

Some of the names used in this book derive from legend and lore. Other names reference family members, parishioners, and friends. The name, *John Gilbert*, is used to honor the author's longtime family and personal friend, J. Gilbert Kaufman of Lewes, Delaware. The town of Saxonburg in Butler County, Pennsylvania, was chosen by the author as the model for the setting of this story. Holy Trinity Church is totally fictious. This church does not, and has never existed in the town of Saxonburg.

This book shares a four-fold dedication. First of all, this book is dedicated to Mr. David Wayne Freehling. Mr. Freehling is a peer of mine and my ace mechanic. People like David are among the unsung heroes of this life who go about their work with skill, fortitude, and dedication. David deserves recognition for his lifetime contribution of automotive service and help to others. For many years I have affectionately called David, "Father Dave". The "circle of wisdom" that is shared each morning by people who stop in to drink some coffee, eat some donuts, and share in conversation I have termed the "Natrona Heights Philosophy Center." David's service and friendship, and that of his late father, Mr. Wayne E. "Buck" Freehling (1927-2000) and his uncle, Mr. Lysle Warren Freehling (1925-2012), have been truly extraordinary throughout seven decades to my family and to me. The character of Father David Freeman in this book is named with Mr. Freehling in mind.

Secondly, I wish to dedicate this book to Mr. Jeffrey Andrew Yeager. Jeff and I befriended each other at Westminster College in Lawrence County, Pennsylvania, during our freshman orientation. We became roommates during our junior and senior years. We have maintained our friendship over many miles and decades. Jeff is an extremely talented individual in many areas of human endeavor. As a retired music teacher, he has served education and the Church of

Jesus Christ with great passion and skill. He is as fine an individual as there is on the planet. I am indebted to him in terms of his help with this book, but also with my 2020 book, *Mary Magdalene: New Testament Eve,* and *Youth Groups My Way: Philosophy, Application, and Anthology.*

Thirdly, I wish to dedicate this book to my family while growing up. My parents, Robert C. Malcolm III and Barbara S. Malcolm; my grandmother, Elvira Toward Malcolm Smith; my great aunts, Mary Edna Tench Stuart and Janet Isabella Malcolm; and my great uncle, George Donnell Stuart, all contributed to making the holiday season very special for my brother, W. Stuart Malcolm, my sister, Barbara Ann Malcolm Kennedy, and myself.

Finally, I wish to dedicate this book to all the fine Christian parishioners for whom I had the great pleasure to serve, and with whom I worked in the service of our Lord and Savior. Many of the characters in this book are patterned after the people in the First Presbyterian Church of Bentleyville and the Natrona Heights Presbyterian Church, in both individual and composite ways. These people include, but are not limited to, Fred and Mary Cristina, Helen Greenawalt, Margaret Evans Jacques, Betty Jane Allshouse, Ruth Sleighter, Emily Davis, and Edward Harold Garlitz, Jr. As I write this, please note that the character of Agnes Hecate Heller does not represent a solitary individual, but a composite personality of the people I have met or heard about whose contributions to church membership and service received rather mixed reviews.

It is my hope and prayer that this book will contribute to, and provide encouragement toward the ministry and mission of the Christian Churches as the world deals with the aftermath of the Covid-19 pandemic.

Contents

Preface

When it comes to the holiday season, which for me growing up included everything from Halloween through Epiphany, I was delighted with "scary ghost stories and tales of the glories" of this annual period of time. As a child, I became enchanted with Charles Dickens's "A Christmas Carol." I was first introduced to the tale through the 1962 television cartoon version, "Mister Magoo's Christmas Carol". My family, during my childhood, viewed the presentation every year. As my life progressed, I began to read Dickens's story of Ebenezer Scrooge each Advent. I have also viewed every single movie and broadcast of the story that has been available for purchase on DVD's during the last 25 years. It has always been my hope and dream that someone would write and publish a tale of a Christmas ghost story as wonderful as that of Dickens's work in 1843. I never thought myself capable of writing such a thing. Starting in 2017, the year I retired from the Natrona Heights Presbyterian Church as pastor and youth group leader, I began to think about possible plots for some sort of Christmas ghost story. Dickens wrote many Christmas stories, including ghost stories, but most of them I find difficult to read. I must admit that I lost interest in them and found that they were good to incite a "long winter's nap."

In the autumn of 2019, I found myself seriously contemplating a plot line for a Christmas ghost story. All of a sudden, an idea shot through my brain and the main story line unfolded within my mind. I let the story percolate in my brain for a few weeks. On December 11 of that year, I sat "in the circle of wisdom" (as the waiting area is known) at David Freehling's service station in Natrona Heights. There I took pen and put my ideas to paper while my vehicle was being serviced. This rough outline, character development, and the initial jottings of dialogue were not fleshed out until the autumn of 2020. A rough draft of the novella was produced in late 2020. Following a critical review in which the contents were examined, significant additions were made to the story. This work was completed in early 2021. During this time, the setting of the story was also placed in Western Pennsylvania and included the 2020 Covid-19 pandemic. It was also suggested that the "Pittsburghese" dialect be employed to add some comic relief to the story.

Besides the entertainment value of this story, the purpose of the book is to produce some thought and provide some commentary on the Christian church community during this difficult period of time. Churches in the United States were struggling prior to the pandemic. The pandemic only made things worse. It is the hope of this author that the Christian community recognizes the spiritual struggle that envelops it during this particular time in history. It is hoped that some rethinking of doctrine, praxis, and attitude will lead to some needed changes in the way the Christian community understands its role and task in today's world. It is believed here that the Christian Church must become more Christocentric, re-examining and embracing the theology taught by the Bible, and go forth being truly led by God's "precious Holy Spirit" and not some of the other spirits of this age.

To quote Charles Dickens's preface (December 1843) to *A Christmas Carol In Prose Being A Ghost Story of Christmas*: "I have endeavoured, in this ghostly little book, to raise the Ghost of an Idea, which shall not put my readers out of humour with themselves, with each other, with the season, or with me. May it haunt their houses pleasantly and no one wish to lay it!"

Stave 1

ᏣᎯ The Call of the Spirit

he child, Rasmus Gilbert Feynman, never dreamed of serving as a clergyman. The prospect of being a priest had never even tempted his young mind. Therefore, he didn't contemplate it as a possibility at all. His parents were a church-going couple who were deeply invested in the Episcopal Church in America and all things divine. They were third generation Americans whose families emigrated from Dudley, England and the Tippermuir area of Scotland. Embracing family values and traditions from the old country, they made sure that their family was duly educated in the faith through the exercise of instruction both at home and in the church. They were strict with their children, but very loving as well. It was a quality childhood for Rasmus and his brother and sister. To young Rasmus a career in the Church was completely out of the question. Heaven, however, had others plans as, in time, became most evident. That Rasmus received a personal invitation by God to serve God in this clerical capacity was something not welcomed by his person. He went fighting and kicking and arguing and debating with the Spirit of God and within himself until, wondrously and amazingly, he found himself ordained as an Anglican priest.

Looking back, Rasmus always wondered just how it had all happened. The call to become a priest, like many other professional callings in this world, was something that Rasmus believed one must never enter into either with speed or enthusiasm. He believed a person should only pursue this calling if it was discovered that one could do no other. In other words, after exhausting all the reasons not to pursue this ecclesiastical profession, Rasmus had finally to embrace it as God's will, but not until he was deep into his seminary education. Yes, the battle within himself and with Providence lasted a long time.

During his wrestling with the divine will, Rasmus' favorite three biblical characters became Moses, Thomas, and Paul. Like Moses, Rasmus made several attempts trying to change God's mind concerning the plans God had for him. Rasmus noted the fact that God became angry with Moses. This ended Moses' futile efforts to deny his call and wiggle out of the work God had in store for him. Learning from Moses' experience, Rasmus decided not to belabor the issue. Rasmus could also identify with the person of Thomas, who was given the moniker of "The Doubter". Rasmus thought that Thomas' identification with doubt was an unfortunate one. It was not that Rasmus doubted his Christian faith, but he believed that faith had to have a proper intellectual foundation. Rasmus found Thomas' search for evidence quite compelling; so much so that Thomas became his favorite saint. As for Paul who was blinded in his opposition to the resurrected Christ, Rasmus found the apostle's three-year sabbatical in the desert to study and contemplate prior to the conduct of ministry quite appropriate. Rasmus affirmed both a studied and prayerful approach to ministry.

Finally, being at peace with his calling, Rasmus prepared for a lifetime of service as an Anglican rector. That, however, is getting ahead of our story. Rasmus discovered that the occupation chosen for him was a significant non-starter when it came to dating and eventually finding a life partner. While most young women admired his convictions, they did not want to subject themselves to a life as a minister's wife. Ministry was not financially lucrative. It was also time consuming and brought with it so many unreasonable expectations for a clergyperson's spouse. The fact that one was in the public eye and could become a target for excessive gossip and possible derision was just too much to contemplate for many a young lady.

Rasmus was fortunate, maybe we should refer to it as blessed, to come into the acquaintance of a young woman named Laurel. He met her at a church social event in the Pittsburgh area for people in his age range. This occurred in the middle of his seminary experience. It was a game night. He, and this young lady he took an immediate liking to, squared off in game after game enjoying both the competition and their lively banter. He was instantly taken by her and determined to get to know her better. She was enrolled at Westminster College in New Wilmington, Pennsylvania, studying education at the time they met. Her desire was to become a teacher.

Laurel was a bright and cheerful individual. She was not only physically attractive, but she also possessed a personality to which people gravitated. She had an engaging smile and hazel eyes that sparkled in the light. Her beautiful long brown hair had just enough of a curl to present quite a fashionable look. A bit mysterious and alluring, she could easily captivate a young man's fancy. Most of all, she was a kind and compassionate individual whose heart was full of love for God's own. One could say that she was a good person; at least as far as human beings this side of Eden could possibly be. Rasmus not only found her to be delightful, but he sensed that there was something very singular about her. Yes, there was something about her that was beyond what one would identify as good, wholesome, admirable, and excellent. She possessed some remarkable quality that was difficult to describe. She embodied and expressed all of the aforementioned qualities and still more.

Laurel was not without options for male companionship in life. Many men were attracted to her and desired to get to know her better. She, however, spurned them all looking for a man she could really connect with on a deeper personal level. She was looking for a man who would be absolutely faithful, exceedingly loyal, and ever trustworthy. The man she wanted was one she could confide in, one who would be honest with her, and a person who would treasure all her thoughts, opinions, and expressions within his heart. She was also interested in a lifetime partner who shared her spiritual convictions.

While the name Rasmus was a strange appellation to many, Laurel found it rather enchanting as if it were derived from a fairy tale. She found Rasmus to be an endearing and energetic individual. He was romantic and creative in the way he courted her. She came to believe that life with him would not only be fun but an adventure as well. Rasmus was not an overly handsome man. He was of average height and rather slender. He possessed dark brown hair and sported a mustache in his early adult years. What he did possess was a good heart full of love for God and God's people. He affirmed Biblical dictates and attempted to live his life informed by Christian principles. He was polite and appropriate in both his mannerisms and speech. He was a true gentleman and just the kind of man for whom Laurel was looking. For Rasmus and Laurel the attraction was almost instantaneous. Quickly, Rasmus' infatuation with her blossomed into love. Before the evening of their first encounter with each other was over, Rasmus asked her out. She was quick to respond in the affirmative. Their growing love and regard for each other advanced rapidly. Neither wanted the other to get away and so a quick and early engagement was the order of the day. Their betrothal was a short one much to the dismay of Laurel's parents. They privately hoped she would have chosen a man with greater professional aspirations.

Although a resident of Delmont, Pennsylvania, Christmas season nuptials were exchanged at Laurel's childhood home church, Saint Alban's Anglican Church in nearby Murrysville. It was a beautiful wedding for a very handsome couple. Both Laurel and Rasmus finished their educational pursuits. Rasmus graduated from the Trinity School for Ministry down the Ohio river from Pittsburgh, was ordained, and then secured his first parish assignment. Things went well at this church, establishing Rasmus as an up-and-coming priest holding much promise for the future. The couple found themselves delighted with their union. Their love quickly produced two children: John Gilbert and Janet Isabella. Not long after the birth of their daughter, Rasmus became the rector of Holy Trinity Church in the town of Saxonburg in Western Pennsylvania.

Saxonburg was not a large town, but had an almost magical feel to it. It was a rather quaint village with an old-time look and many pleasing shops. It was not a town, however, altogether caught in yesteryear. True, it was surrounded by a farming community, but it did have some light industry and employment was plentiful at this time in the area. Rasmus and Laurel loved both the rural and small town feel to their new home. The opportunity for her to pursue a future teaching career in this locale when her children became older also appeared, much to her delight, to be a distinct possibility.

The church was a large one considering the size of the community. It had the appearance of being quite ancient. It certainly was the largest building in the village. Its size and magnificence were not without purpose and plan. A very wealthy benefactor had underwritten the construction of this grand edifice in memory of his late wife. She was, in fact, entombed in the church in a special room off the sanctuary where later her husband came to rest beside her. Due to his generosity the church was also financially well endowed. The church itself harkened back to an era in time when the church tower or steeple was the tallest object on the immediate horizon. This was no mistake in the architecture of bygone days. A person could see the top of the spire from any location within the town. It was also easily identifiable in a distance from any point in the farming district surrounding it. The church was a place of great inspiration to the people and served as a community center for its citizens. It was much loved.

Upon his arrival, Rasmus launched immediately into his responsibilities. He was almost tireless in the way he pursued getting to know the congregants and providing additional opportunities for programming and worship. Little by little the church began to grow numerically. Little by little the church found itself center stage in the lives of many of its parishioners and attendees. Little by little the sensation of a sweet spirit filled the building with the joy of the Lord. While not everything Rasmus pursued for the church worked out well, the people were most pleased with his effort and imagination. Despite some minor setbacks along the way, the church was becoming a source of much godly inspiration for people in the community. This may be an odd thing to say, but the church's spiritual advancement was attracting some undue notice. The progress of the church was not only perceived by heaven, but by heaven's adversaries as well. It attracted the attention of all beings both good and evil. Rasmus did have some human detractors. They, however, were kept at bay by the support of many fine people who were pleased with his ministry and the ascendency of the church. This, of course, had to change according to those entities who delighted in spoiling all things godly.

The years passed quickly as Rasmus and Laurel enjoyed the church, the community, their children, and their great love for each other early in their Holy Trinity Church experience. As the children grew, they added a canine to the family; an American Staffordshire Terrier whom they named "Kinghorn." Kinghorn was a stray who wandered into the church one summer Sunday and walked down the aisle right to Rasmus in the pulpit. He seemed taken with the preacher and would not leave his side much to the amusement of the congregation. Without any identification and unable to locate his owner the Feynmans made him part of their family. The children loved and enjoyed the dog, but Kinghorn's foremost loyalty and affection was focused on Rasmus. Rasmus affectionately referred to him as his "brindle buddy."

All was well and promising until the dawn of one bright and sunny day deep in December…

"Good morning, my dear," expressed Rasmus to Laurel as he filled a cup with coffee and sat down at the table. The ever-present Kinghorn followed him into the breakfast room and took his customary place by his side.

"You appear to be in an exceptionally good mood this morning, my love," replied Laurel.

"You are correct," affirmed Rasmus. "I enjoy this season immensely and we have a great one shaping up in the church this Advent. I am very excited about the church's prospects as we close out this year and advance into the next. In addition,

I failed to share with you the substance of my meeting with Edward Garland the other day."

"He was so energized to share some ideas with you. What is it all about?" asked Laurel.

"My dear, the good news from this meeting is that he wants to help me manage my duties in this parish," responded Rasmus. "He sees, as the church grows, how much of my time is taken up with organizational tasks. He wants to help relieve me of some of these to allow me to have more time for mission and ministry, as well as more time with you and the children."

"That is wonderful, Rasmus," stated Laurel excitedly. "He is a good man with marvelous sensibilities. His reasoning, knowing him, must be pure. God bless him! He sees a need and it is one he has the time and talent to remedy. God bless him again I say!"

"I have to believe," asserted Rasmus, "that God must be involved in providing another blessing and a greater opportunity to advance the divine will and purpose in this place. I will share with you the details in which he and I agreed very soon, my dear. Of course, everything is contingent upon a favorable review by and the approval of the Vestry."

"When will all this begin?" asked Laurel.

"We hope to pursue this in the new year. We hope to have everything operational sometime this winter." replied Rasmus. "Now it is time to eat this delicious breakfast you have prepared and then I have got to get to the office. I have many appointments today and I would like to finish the message for the 'Eve of the Eve' service as well.

"How are your preparations for Christmas Eve going?" asked Laurel.

"I already have the service and message finished for Christmas Eve." responded Rasmus.

"I admire you Rasmus", stated Laurel, "for always being prepared, and especially being ready in advance during this season so that the pressure on you is manageable."

"Thank you, my dear!" stated Rasmus with appreciation. "I do not like to do things under the pressure afforded by the calendar and the clock."

At this point John Gilbert and Janet Isabella joined their father and mother at the table as they were preparing for another day's adventure in their early education.

"Good morning Daddy," exclaimed John and Janet nearly in unison.

"Good morning children," cried their father. "I hope you have a good day and learn lots of important things at school."

"Some of the things they teach us – well - I do not understand how they will ever matter to us." John expressed.

"That's because you are not as bright as I am in every subject," teased Janet.

"I'm smarter than you are in the things that matter," countered John.

"You are just jealous because I am a better student and I get higher grades!" snapped Janet. With that Janet raised her foot attempting to place it between John's face and his bowl of cereal as they sat near each other at the corner of the table.

John swatted it away yelling, "Cut that out!"

"Mommy," cried Janet, "Johnny hit me!"

"I saw what you did. Now stop it both of you," replied their mother.

After consuming a full breakfast, Rasmus waited until his children went out the door on their walk to school. He said good-bye to both of them and gave them a great big hug.

"What is on the agenda for your day, dear?" he asked.

"I have got some household chores to do and some baking for the holiday to accomplish. I also need to finish wrapping presents and put the final touches on holiday plans and decorations. I think it will be a fun day. One other thing I will accomplish today is getting my application finished. I sure hope I can secure the teaching position that is opening up at the elementary school as we have previously discussed," Laurel responded.

"That's fine. Good luck getting everything done today, but please remember to enjoy yourself in this season. Don't work too hard," replied Rasmus.

He then kissed his wife on her cheek and patted Kinghorn on his head. At that he was off down the walkway and around the corner to Holy Trinity. Living on parish property adjacent to the church was beneficial, but sometimes easy access to the pastor and his family was all too convenient. Church members often intruded on Rasmus at home. This, during certain seasons of the year, became an annoyance. It was one, however, the family tolerated with the state of the church being so bright and promising.

Rasmus had a very full agenda for the day. Not only did he have service preparations to make, but he had people to counsel and the ill to visit. He also had a couple of recommendation letters to write and some correspondence with which to deal. He hoped he could carve out some time in the day to continue working on the Bible class he was planning to teach in the upcoming year. The day was an ordinary one which gave no hint to the grave things that were soon to come to pass – for Rasmus, for his family, and for the church.

Rasmus returned to the rectory promptly at 5 o'clock in the afternoon. Supper was served at 5:30. Rasmus had to go back to the church for his evening appointments by 6:30. He thoroughly enjoyed his table time with his family. He listened to their narrative of the events of the day and laughed at their observations. He informed them that he would try to be home early to continue reading the seasonal bed-time stories. That was one of his tasks in the family. It was one he found most enjoyable and his children looked forward to this experience as well. Little did anyone know what was about to transpire and how it would change their lives forever.

Stave 2
The Little Girl

Departing from his office following an evening's work, Rasmus smiled as he looked forward to this night's homecoming. He was content in the knowledge that his dedication to God was serving his church and its people well. He loved the Lord and God's people. He exercised an undying dedication, possessed a seemingly limitless imagination, and displayed an unquenchable energy. This you must know for sometimes in the divine realm the essence of a faithful steward and quality under-shepherd to the Great Shepherd of us all, can be translated into a manifestation by divine decree from beyond the grave for God's special purposes. Of course, this possibility is known to few and even realized by less!

Rector Feynman enjoyed his ministry. He also enjoyed the beautiful Gothic architecture of the church he served. Its architecture sported a tall commanding bell tower with a large stone cross balanced on its pinnacle. The parish employed a custodial team who took care of the building and its grounds. It was well known to everyone, however, that the good Rector also treated the church with a caring touch. He oversaw all the church appointments. He made sure everything in the church was in good order and in its proper place. He also acted as a night watchman. He made late nightly rounds to guarantee that all lights were turned off, and all doors which needed locking were secure. It is on such a night, while making his tour of the building, that the events which led to his earthly demise transpired. In fact, it was on Saint Thomas' Day. This day was celebrated by the Anglican Church on December 21. Rasmus enjoyed the story of Thomas' great confession of the Christ and his discovery of new life in Jesus. He envisioned the feast of St. Thomas as a prelude to all things heavenly and eternal. It must be noted that it was on this particular day that Father Feynman met a tragic earthly and physical end. Perhaps in the great scheme of things this can be looked back upon as being suitable, but for the church and those who loved him it was most untimely, shocking, and full of grief and sorrow.

Late on this feast day in Advent, Rasmus was doing what he always did each and every night – inspecting the building to make sure that everything was in good condition and properly secured. Exiting the nave to the right of the altar, he noticed a glimmer of light coming up from the descending stairwell. He was puzzled, in large part, because he did not notice this light at the start of his walkthrough. He presumed that the glowing radiance was located at the entrance to the undercroft or fellowship hall. Running down the staircase and rounding the corner to his left, he was startled to spy a young child standing in the threshold of an open door. This was the door to a storage room which had once been the base of a now dismantled stairway and street exit. The child was a girl of perhaps eight or nine years. She wore a light blue and white dress from yesteryear. Her freckled face was bracketed by long dish-water blond hair cascading downward covering her ears. She sported a broad, friendly grin directed at the Rector. Rasmus was stunned to see her. In his surprise he uttered not a word of inquiry. In what seemed like a long period of time to Rasmus, but was nothing more than mere seconds, the stationary little girl began to walk out from the doorway and turned. Still smiling at him, she disappeared into a small adjacent room to her left. Rasmus followed rapidly. Deliberately, he turned on the lights and the power switches to all the small rooms and closets he passed by while moving down the hallway. He wanted as much illumination as he could achieve. He entered the cavity and turned on the light. To his great surprise he discovered that the room was completely empty. The little girl was not to be found! He did notice, however, that the air in the room was strangely cold. This was a bitter cold which he had never experienced inside the church before. Exiting the chilly room, he was perplexed and perturbed. He immediately started to review the encounter in his mind. This was certainly not a ghost for the little girl standing down the hallway was not transparent.

She was solid. She was physical. She was real. He had seen her with his own two eyes. There was no way, he thought, that she could have been a figment of his imagination. In no way, he assured himself, did his mind and senses conjure her. He was not a person given to flights of fantasy. He had never been involved in any situation like this in his entire life.

As Rasmus entertained his thoughts and sought a rational explanation, he heard a thumping coming from somewhere on the floor above. He ran up the two flights of steps to the sanctuary level. In the dim light his eyes suddenly grew large as a picture on the wall was violently moving back and forth on its placement nail. Quickly it crashed to the floor breaking both the glass and the frame. "What in God's good name is going on here?" he quickly said to himself out loud.

Then, as if to answer his verbal exclamation, he heard an audible voice coming from somewhere on the uppermost floor making a lengthy utterance in the common tongue. The statement was produced by a chilling and terrifying voice. The message was not one he could clearly distinguish. Frightened, but duty driven to secure the building, he raced up to the top of the staircase. Once there, he peered down the hall toward a room whose door stood open. Father Feynman was both puzzled and perplexed. Just a few minutes ago he had shut that door and proceeded to lock it. Walking slowly and observantly to the room, he turned on the light to inspect its contents. Finding no one present there, he deliberately turned off the light and once more shut and locked the door. Beginning his search for what must be an intruder or a person or persons playing an elaborate hoax, a frightened Rasmus began to slowly and cautiously walk down the hallway. As he did so he turned around to glance back at the room he had just vacated. He saw a bright, white light appearing from underneath this very same door. The light beaming out from the bottom of the door travelled a distance on the carpeted floor. Walking slowly, Rasmus returned to that door once more. He unlocked it and opened it for a third time. To his surprise, the room was totally dark possessing no light source at all!

Since this room also contained the staircase to the attic and the tall tower above, he determined to himself to investigate these upper areas of the building. What if trespassers were now present in either of these locations? No one was found in the attic after a diligent search. Ascending the ladder to the tower room he switched on the light. This room contained the wooden pipes of the choir loft organ. In the dimly lit room, the pipes formed oddly shaped shadows on the walls surrounding him. He then advanced carefully toward the spiral staircase. This stairway would take him to the belfry. He moved with caution amid the organ pipes. He stayed away from the baffles. The baffles were a series of slanted boards underneath which was an open and missing floor. The room had been designed and constructed this way to reflect the sound of the pipes downward and out into the sanctuary below.

Suddenly, in the corner from whence he had come, was the same little girl standing there smiling once more at him. As quickly as she appeared, she vanished right before his eyes taking on a shadowy presence. A dark mist rose and expanded in size filling the enormous room from floor to ceiling. The figure of a large entity began to form. The outline of a hideous female face soon took shape and became more distinct. Rasmus was deeply alarmed. Appendages appeared on the phantom forming arms and hands. The macabre figure then lunged at him. It came straight at him as if to grab and envelop him. This caused him to step back quickly once, twice and then again. Without realizing it he was moving toward the open cavity in the room. In his alarm he had forgotten about the gaping hole in the floor. He reached it, and losing his balance began falling backward. Stretching his arms in vain for anything to grasp in order to catch and steady himself, he found nothing in reach to prevent his fall. Down he went more than 75 feet, crashing onto the chancel floor below. His body hit with a deadening thud near the Epistle ambo. The good Rector, bones splintered and his vital organs shredded, lay dead! He was now as inanimate as the wooden furniture around him.

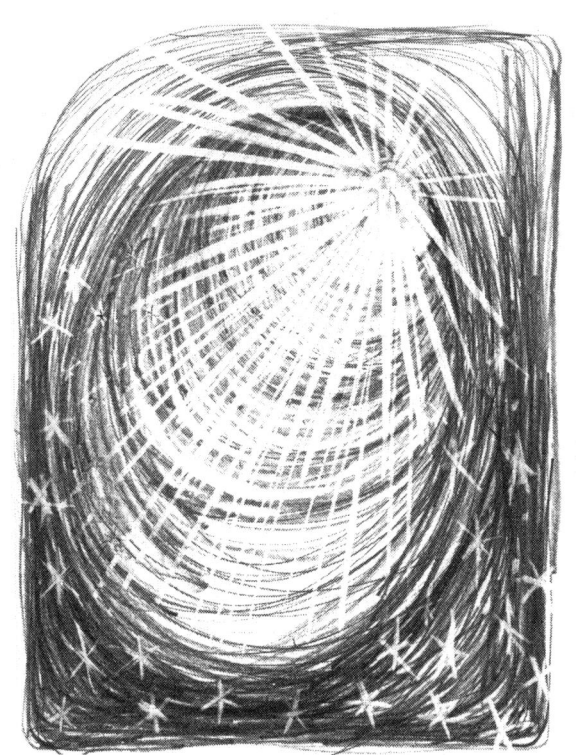

An Unanticipated Assignment

There sprawled out on the chancel floor was the body of Rasmus G. Feynman. His conscious essence peered down in disbelief upon his lifeless body urging his former self to rise up and stand. Quickly he realized that no resuscitation or bodily resurrection was going to occur. The fact of the matter was clear and most evident; he was dead! Yet, he possessed his senses and his ability to think and reason. For a few moments he looked downward trying to come to terms with his fall and the "now what" question that suddenly began to plague his mind. Looking up to where he had fallen from, he noticed a tiny pin point of light growing in brilliance and expanding in size above him. It was an unearthly white light that almost appeared to have a soft texture about it. It was unlike any light and coloration he had ever witnessed in his existence thus far. It was a light to which he was drawn. At the same time, this expanding illumination was moving closer and closer to him.

Slowly, almost imperceptibly, he noticed that he was levitating and travelling upward. Within the beam of light exploding upon his soul and encompassing him, he was now looking down at his body from the upper interior surface of the cavernous sanctuary. Everything was happening so rapidly that the only feelings Rasmus possessed were of deep confusion and profound mystery. Quickly he noticed that he was passing through the ceiling and the various levels of the tower and belfry. Soon he was outside the church. The church, and the town surrounding it, began to miniaturize as the light was transporting him through space and perhaps, time. Travelling faster and faster through a myriad of fancy colors and what he perceived to be passing stars; a great sense of peace and love seemed to wash over his spirit. Then the tunnel of light surrounding him suddenly slowed, bringing him to a beatific vision of a verdant valley with a shining city some distance away. There a road heading toward the city appeared before him. As he began gliding toward the effervescent citadel, he was met by a figure emitting a glowing radiance which made its features difficult to distinguish. A strong voice from this figure bid him to stop.

"Come no closer," stated the being. "Welcome to the Intermediate Heaven and His Majesty's celestial abode! The city beyond is for my Master's saints, servants, and stewards. This city is for the faithful. Please be assured that a place has been reserved in your name. Before you can enter, I must share with you that your time of earthly accomplishment is not yet over. Your work is not complete."

"How can that be?" questioned Rasmus. "Everything has happened so fast. Moments ago, I was alive and now I find myself on the threshold of heaven. I am not sure I understand what has taken place and what is happening now. This whole experience seems to me to be both a nightmare and a wonderful dream. You will need to grant me a greater explanation. I must admit, however, that I am feeling a great welcome and an assurance of well-being at having arrived at this place."

At this Rasmus went on trying to make sense of his new experience based on what he had learned on earth, "I believe that this experience indicates to me that I am dead to my former life. Once deceased, one's physical life is finished until the glorious bodily resurrection of all of Christ's own. Is not that the truth?"

Before the figure could answer, Rasmus continued, "It is the truth I learned from august ministers of the Lord as gleaned from the Holy Word! Once a person has died, I was taught that there is no return to one's former life," expressed Rasmus with conviction.

"That is not entirely correct, my new arrival," the presence answered. "If you will remember in the Word, there are several stories of resuscitation, resurrection, and spirit appearance such as Samuel, Moses, and Elijah. If our Majesty desires someone to return to his or her life, such as Lazarus rising from his tomb to accomplish the divine Will, then what is desired becomes so," stated the radiant entity.

"I had so much more to accomplish in my position," cried Rasmus. "I gave much of my time, resources, and energy to the divine work. I surrendered many of my own interests and relationships to accomplish what I believed was the call of God on my life. Yet looking back, I did not even come close to fulfilling what I desired to secure for the parish I served. While I am happy to be in this marvelous new realm, it is true, I would also welcome a return to finish my work at Holy Trinity Church. May I return to inhabit my body once more and be healed from that terrible fall?"

"Your time for that work is now complete," replied the beaming entity. "You have been a good and faithful servant. You have exercised great stewardship of God's property and people. Be ye well assured, you will be greatly rewarded. This, however, is not a return assignment to that which you previously performed. You are being sent back for a new undertaking with a fresh purpose. Providence has determined that your help is needed to remedy some untoward circumstances in your former charge. This type of commission is most rare. Consider it both a privilege and a bestowal of great favor to be chosen for this work."

"What is it that I am to do? How am I to accomplish it seeing that I am dead to my former life and position?" responded Rasmus.

"You will soon find," stated the radiant figure, "that two whole years have transpired since your tragic demise. "I am sending you back to what for you would be an earthly future. Do not be alarmed for time here in this realm is much different from that with which you are accustomed. In your place a new rector has been elected. His name is Father David Freeman. He, like you, possesses a heart for God and God's people. Yet, things are not well with him or the church. What you were unaware of in the December of your earthly demise was that a global pandemic was about to sweep over the entire sphere. It would be much like the one during and following the end of the Great War. Many people would become ill. Many people, especially the elderly, would die. In order to attempt to slow the rapid spread of the disease many businesses were shuttered, people were laid off from work, schools were closed, and the travel industry came to near ruin. Churches suffered through this as well. Worship services, church educational courses, and fellowship events were cancelled for long periods of time. Keeping people separated and away from each other ruled those days. The financial hardship was significant. What was even more grave was the fact that people became comfortable with life without church. Many of them did not return after a vaccine was administered. This is the situation you will find yourself in upon your re-entry. So significant was the pandemic that it gave evil a great opportunity with which to play. At Holy Trinity Church many people are murmuring against Father Freeman and are failing to give him the proper support he needs to conduct his work and fulfill his calling. Sadly, many people no longer care. Despite the utilization of cyberspace and other media of communication and contact, gathering God's family together again has taken a giant step backwards. Besides that, the evil specter that caused your death is still resident in the building and needs to be removed. With all the terrible happenings since your own personal demise; global circumstances have only fed the apparition's growth. It is now more contemptible and terrifying than during your first encounter. It has become a formidable adversary, but not one in which you, with the help of Providence, cannot overcome. Your assignment is to rally the people and to deliver the church from this evil."

"How am I to accomplish all this?" cried Rasmus.

"You will be given the supernatural enabling you need to conduct your work and bring it to a swift and successful conclusion," remarked the being. "You will be given the power to manipulate your environment. You will be able to see and hear things beyond all barriers. You will be able to visualize the evil specter haunting the church. You will have the ability of movement and instantaneous transportation. Gravity and physical barriers will not prohibit the exercise of your work. You will be able to be present and yet unseen. You can appear to those for whom an encounter with you is necessary. In other words, you will be able to be seen and communicate with the human beings selected as part of your assignment. Providence will not hold back the tools you need to carry out and complete your mission. This includes, the power of the Spirit to free the church from this evil entity. You will soon discover God's method and power to liberate Holy Trinity Church."

"I am ready to take up this task as the Lord wills it," Rasmus confidently exclaimed.

"That is all well and good," replied the being. "You must accomplish this assignment by Christmas Day. The church is still hurting greatly over your demise and it has cast a pall over the Advent season. The new rector is very discouraged and depressed. If things do not appear to be turning around by the size of the attendance at service on Christmas Eve, he plans to resign. First, you will visit four people known to you. On the 21st, you will appear to Helen Greenfield during her morning prayers. She is much discouraged. On the afternoon of the 22nd, you will visit Margaret Jackman whom you will find thoroughly depressed and rather despondent. On the morning of the 23rd, you will attempt to re-energize and re-new God's call upon the life of Edward Garland. Finally, on the evening of the 23rd, you will haunt your main detractor in life, the person of Agnes Hecate Heller. You will seek in her a change of heart concerning her person, and also a new perspective on her service, work, and mission."

"But what precisely am I to say and with what arguments do I share?" pleaded Rasmus.

"All things will become evident to you at the time you initiate each encounter," pronounced the shining representative of heaven.

"There is just one more thing, kind sir," Rasmus stated quickly. "What about my family? I would like to visit them and let them know that my destiny is the company of heaven. Is that possible? I would like them to know that I am fine. I also want to know if they survived the pandemic. Is it well with them?

"Are you talking about your immediate family?" inquired the spirit.

"Yes, I am," responded Rasmus.

"I believe that you have a wife and two children," declared the spirit. "Let me see. Yes, your former wife's name is Laurel."

"There is nothing 'former' about it," snapped Rasmus. "Yes, my wife's name is Laurel."

Continuing, the spirit announced, "And you have a son. His name is John Gilbert. You also have a daughter. Her name is Janet Isabella."

"Once more, good spirit, you are correct," Rasmus affirmed.

The heavenly being continued, "Your assignment is one that is most rare. Sending a soul back to earth on mission does not happen very often. The parameters of your orders are quite narrow. I am sorry, but you may not make contact with your family. As much as this may cause you pain, it is the way it is in the heavenly realm. People do not return to be with family. Instead, loved ones join those who precede them. They arrive into the glad tidings of the intermediate heaven prior to the coming fullness of the new heaven and new earth. Your Bible gives instruction on such matters. Does it not?"

"Yes, it does," Rasmus said sadly. "Could you please make an exception just this one time?"

"There is a reason for this, you must understand, even if I cannot give you a full explanation now. Allow me to clarify things once more. Such an encounter is not a part of your instructions. I cannot make an exception in your case. I am, in fact, not allowed to make an exception in your case. An appearance by you to your family is not permitted," charged the heavenly being. "It is not up to me. I am just passing along to you the current calling upon your soul. Trust that Providence will take care of everything else. You cannot reveal yourself to them. You may only reveal yourself to those with whom you have been instructed to visit."

"What about their welfare?" retorted Rasmus. "Have they fallen to the pandemic?"

"This I can tell you," exclaimed his radiance. "They are all alive and well. The pandemic did not touch them!"

"God be praised!" responded Rasmus with relief.

"Now to the exercise of your assignment. You may carry on!" With these parting words the divine entity disappeared.

The next thing that Rasmus knew, he found himself located in the lofty tower of Holy Trinity Church once more.

The immense steeple with his ponderous cross towered above him. He looked out the open belfry from whence he could see every part of his former hometown. He knew that Father Freeman would be occupying the rectory at this time. He wondered where his wife and two children might have relocated. He wondered if they were still living in the town. He was displeased with himself for failing to ask this question of God's spokes-agent. He wondered if they might have left Saxonburg, taking up residence with or near Laurel's parents. If he couldn't reveal himself to them, he would at least like to see them. His heart ached for them and all they had to suffer. His love for them was enormous, but as things were there was nothing he could do about it. In his mind, however, he held out hope that God would somehow, someway, grant him a special dispensation. Maybe a special grace would be bestowed on him at the conclusion of his assignment. He could at least hope that perhaps this might be the case. In the midst of thinking about his wife and children he reminded himself that he had more pressing matters of which to concern himself.

Swooping down in an instant to the front of the church he read the decorative Advent calendar which was positioned in the yard each year near the marquee. Sure enough, it read December 21. It was indeed, Saint Thomas' Day – precisely two years from the day of that terrible occurrence which ended his previous life. On the church sign he noted that the next advertised service was on Christmas Eve. He had this day and two more to complete his new heavenly assignment!

Stave 4
The First Visit

Rasmus returned to the church tower and continued to enjoy the sights and sounds of an earthly morning. He delighted in watching the rising sun and the birds take to flight. He enjoyed listening to the advancing noise of the town as it awakened and found its voice. Possessing the gift of an internal clock, Rasmus knew the time for his first visit was drawing nigh. Taking to flight he flew through the streets to a residence he knew well – the cottage of Helen Greenfield.

Helen was a single woman in her mid-eighties who had never married. Rumor has it that she once was in love, but the object of her affection died in combat in service to the country. Heartbroken, she apparently never made a love connection again as far as Rasmus knew. While she had some friends within the church, she kept mostly to herself and to her extended family. She loved her siblings and nieces and nephews. As the family expanded, she came to enjoy her great nieces and nephews. Helen had served as a librarian for a major corporation's research and development facility in the area. She was a very focused individual who took her faith seriously. An observer would not identify her as a religious zealot. Her faith expression was not particularly verbal. She was, however, a person of deep devotion and contemplation most mindful of the spiritual disciplines. She was not openly warm. It took a while to break through the barriers of unknowing to develop a relationship with her. Once a relationship was forged, she displayed the attributes of empathy, sympathy, compassion, and kindness. She had been a very handsome woman in her younger days, but now the ravages of age had taken their toll on her youthful beauty. While her hearing was still sharp, her vision had to be aided by constant adjustments to her spectacles.

Helen was enjoying her two-hour morning prayer and devotional time. Sitting comfortably in her living room drinking a cup of tea with her Bible by her side, Helen was fumbling through a stack of papers, letters, cut out articles, and pages of extensive prayer listings. Most of her prayer lists were from former days of heightened church activity and community contact.

Invisibly, Rasmus entered her presence through a wooden framed glass window. He observed that her quaint cottage sitting room was sparsely decorated for Christmas. A thin and deteriorating three-foot artificial tree was the only reminder that it was the holiday season. Rasmus sat down on an old soft chair just opposite Helen. Slowly, he materialized calling out to her softly.

"Helen, Helen, do not be afraid! It's me, Father Feynman."

With this manifestation, Helen's tea went flying across the room. Her cup hit a vase and sent it crashing to the floor. All her papers were tossed in the air and floated down like so much confetti.

"Helen, Helen, please forgive me for giving you such a fright. Please settle yourself", cried Rasmus in an attempt to comfort her. "I know not how to make my initial appearance to you more palatable."

"Who are you? What are you? What is the meaning of this disturbance?" shouted Helen in nearly a complete panic.

"Believe me Helen, I am who I say I am – Father Feynman. I am not some malevolent phantom or an evil entity. I am not a figment of your imagination. It's your old friend and former priest Rasmus. I have been sent back into your world on mission from our beloved Majesty. My spirit is taking on the form of an apparition of my former self so that you may know the validity of which I speak. It is really me, Helen," stated Rasmus.

Still in shock and suffering from a good dose of panic, Helen had enough soundness of mind to cry out, "Depart from me spirit! Away with you! Go back to the pit of hell from which you came! I say this in the precious name of Jesus my Lord and my Savior."

"Helen, I am telling you the truth, it's really me," asserted Rasmus. "I am the one in this life whom you dearly loved, supported, and enjoyed! You are a beloved saint dear to my heart. Your daily prayers for me, when I was with you in this world, produced a great harvest. You are one of many individuals who helped to produce a sweet spirit among those in our church family. Your love for God and God's people kept much evil at bay. You prayed for the growth of our congregation both in terms of the spirit and people in the pews. You were a great Christian sister to me as we worked together side by side. Do you now believe that it is me? Do you believe my word that I have been sent by God?"

'Yes, your appearance and words seem to be that of my old friend," Helen spoke cautiously. Still trembling slightly, she asked, "How can this be? How is it you have come back from the dead? Please tell me! Once deceased, I thought that a soul could never return!"

Responding to her inquiry, Rasmus continued, "This is a rare and direct act of God. I assure you that I am who I say I am and not something untoward. Please note in your Bible that God has accomplished this before. This is another way in which God works and communicates with God's own. It is, I must admit, quite unusual."

"Is it well with you, Helen?" asked Rasmus. "How do you fare these days?"

"I am doing as well as a woman my age can possibly do. Fortunately, I have been blessed with a good constitution and have thus far avoided the more significant ravages of clock and calendar. It is kind of you to ask. You did not come here to inquire of my well-being, so get on with it. Tell me why are you here? Why have you come to me? What is your purpose? What do you want from me?" exclaimed Helen as she raised her voice.

'Helen," responded Rasmus, "I have been informed that you have stopped attending worship services and serving the Lord through your active presence and participation."

"It is not my church anymore," Helen emphatically stated in an assertive voice.

"What do you mean, it is not your church anymore?" inquired Rasmus.

"I don't know the people who worship with me," said Helen. "There were so many new people attending the church at the time of your death. I have nothing in common with them. They do not know me and I do not know them. With your death and the onslaught of the pandemic, very few people attend services these days. Among those who still do, I recognize very few. Like I said, It's just not my church anymore!"

"Helen, don't you see that your prayers to fill the church have been answered. You have labored for years, wrestling with the Holy Spirit to bless this congregation. One could see your prayers coming true in the weeks and months just prior to my death. Worship services were full, lively, and vibrant! As I looked out over the congregation, I saw many smiling and happy faces during those days. You've been blessed and God has answered your prayers in a demonstrative and marvelous way. God has heard you and responded. You have not only been blessed, but your work has blessed the church and many people as well," cried Rasmus

"I don't feel blessed," mumbled Helen. "They are all aliens to me. No, I am done with this church!"

Rasmus became more direct. "Helen, you have lived a long time. You never married. You have few kinfolk. You have become a solitary woman. Most of your friends are no longer among the living. You need to introduce yourself to people. You need to again take up your ministry of prayer. You need to learn about these brothers and sisters of ours and pray for them. Ask them if you can lift their petitions and requests to heaven. Get to know them. Help them. Create a new list with their names and concerns on it. Just as I once prepared prayer lists for you to intercede with God, create your own congregational listing."

Rasmus adjusted himself in the chair, moving closer to Helen. "Helen, I need your help. I have been sent by heaven to renew your call to pray. A malevolent spirit has taken advantage of a growing vacuum in the church. It feeds and expands off a decline in the spiritual fervor of God's people. My death seems to have contributed to this vile circumstance. This spirit is one of destruction. The plan is to occupy the entire edifice, chasing away all the faithful. You need to take up prayer again for the church. You need to activate this call to spiritual warfare. If you start praying for the church and its people again – if you start attending again – if you start serving again, you can help defeat this entity. This foul spirit, Helen, is from the very pit of hell. It is an enemy that must be defeated. God needs you to begin right now. Start by attending the service on Christmas Eve. The new rector, Father Freeman, needs your help. He is young and inexperienced. He needs time to grow and learn. He will make mistakes. His heart, however, is full of love for God and God's people. He is a person of joy and most dedicated to the Lord. Peace needs to be brought to and abide once more in our beloved church. It is your church. You have more claim to the spiritual ownership of that congregation than many of your fellow parishioners. Will you help fulfill the vision? Will you? Will you, please? Can I now count on you? If this wasn't important would I be sitting here sent to you in this very extraordinary manner? I hope you will! I pray you will!"

"Do you know what I fear, Rasmus?" asked Helen.

"No, I do not," replied Rasmus.

"I fear being shelved by God," continued Helen.

"What do you mean by being shelved?" inquired Rasmus.

"Being shelved is a term I have heard people use. It refers to failing to do the work the Lord desires you to perform. In time, as you continually resist God's will, God may decide to put you on the shelf and pay you no or little attention as if you are good for nothing. This can change, of course, if one repents their inactivity and gets involved with the things of the divine again. Rasmus, I think that this is what you are telling me. Maybe I have placed myself on the shelf. Perhaps I need to dust myself off and get busy again," contemplated Helen.

"I think you have made an accurate assessment of the situation," responded Rasmus hopefully. "This is good news to my ears."

"I do have a personal question to inquire of you," added Rasmus. "Do you know the whereabouts of my wife and children?"

"Vaguely," answered Helen. "I believe they moved in with your mother-and father-in-law. They relocated some months following your death."

"Thank you for this information, Helen. You have provided me a great comfort," Rasmus said cheerfully and with a sigh of relief.

"It is time for me to depart," announced Rasmus. "You will see me no more until that day you enter your reward. The amount of blessedness you will receive in the life to come will be determined in part by how you respond and serve in this critical moment. Do not faint in taking up this mission. Good-bye Helen! I will certainly miss you. Thank you for all your prayers on my behalf. I also appreciate your prayers for my wife and family. Please lift up the church in your supplications. Please know that on Christmas Eve I will be watching, and even beyond, for all I know. I trust that you will make the correct decision in this matter. God bless you and your service in this critical hour."

Rasmus took his leave and faded away as if evaporating into the air.

Stave 5

An Unexpected Encounter

In some respects, Father Feynman enjoyed the invisibility of his spiritual essence as he traversed the streets and fields of his former home village. Movement, the former rector discovered, was effortless. He found it amusing to enter shops watching people barter and trade, examine and purchase, eat and drink. He invited himself into his favorite tavern, appropriately named "The Village Tavern", and found his usual seat unoccupied. He wished he had the ability to partake once more of his favorite libation, but this was not one of the special abilities with which he had been graced. His eyes, however, spied a shiny metal plate attached to the table which read: "The Father Rasmus G. Feynman Memorial Table." It was inscribed with the dates of his rectorship at Holy Trinity and his favorite verses from Philippians 3:10 and 11 which reads: "I want to know Christ and the power of his resurrection and the fellowship of sharing in his sufferings, becoming like him in his death, and so, somehow, to attain the out-resurrection from the dead." Sitting down, he looked through the large glass window before him where he could view all the comings and going in this part of town. Silent in observation, he found it easy and rather delightful to eavesdrop on many of the conversations going on around him. Tempted to respond on occasion, he refrained from uttering a single word. Though many a conversation brought him mirth, he kept in check his desire to burst out in laughter. As afternoon passed into evening on the 21st, he found solace sitting near the great fire of the town's only up- scale inn. The fireplace roared much to his delight as the blaze danced enthusiastically, putting on its own visual and auditory spectacle. It helped him chase away from his mind the events of this very night two years previously. Strange as it may seem, he could sense the warmth of the flames which seemed to invigorate his soul. Yet as the evening progressed, he succumbed to melancholy, knowing that he should not, and being under precise instructions, could not, interact with those whom he knew and loved as he did prior to his untimely demise. His sorrow was also enhanced, knowing that he would not encounter his wife and children. It left him yearning, wanting to know everything about their lives. Leaving behind the glad and bright conflagration, he travelled slowly from the lodge on the lamp lit streets and entered his former parish. He tarried in the sanctuary, looking at the dim lights and the shadowy reflections coming through the stained glass.

Having yet to encounter the Lady of the Church, as Rasmus now referred to the evil entity present there, he ascended the tower intent on spending the night much like a watchman keeping guard over all that his vision could observe. As Rasmus settled into the belfry, he felt the presence of something wicked in the air near him. In the opposite corner, on the other side of the church's great bell, he spied a dark hooded figure. The personage was rather diminutive in stature. It barely was visible against the backdrop of the dark night. Nothing of a face or hands were visible. It was a form shrouded in mystery. It was chilling and would produce dread in any human heart. Rasmus knew instantly that the presence was the evil entity haunting the church. This was the same vile specter that had procured his death two years ago this very night.

"What are you doing here?" queried Rasmus assertively.

In a very raspy low voice, which would be most discomforting to human ears, the figure spoke., "Get out! Depart from these premises. This is my place now. I own it. You are not welcome here. Depart immediately."

"This church is not owned by you or those you represent. This place belongs to God and God's own. It is you who need to depart – and depart you will," cried Rasmus.

Rasmus, in his ghostly form, did not fear the demonic spirit as he once had when he was human. He knew that the entity had no authority or power over him. He could speak the truth with clarity. In complete confidence of the righteousness of his cause and with heaven supporting him, he could take an immovable stance against this adversary of God and of everything good, righteous, and true.

"Your arrival as the rector of this parish did not foil my plans for this place, it only delayed them," spoke the darkened entity. "It took me some time, but I got rid of you once and I can nullify your influence again. Fate and fortune smiled on me when you did yourself in by falling through the floor. It was not entirely an accident. I carried off that one much to my pleasure."

"You cannot command my departure now. And there is no cavity into which I must evacuate in my current state. It is you who must leave. You have no power here whatsoever," asserted Rasmus.

"I will finish my work of neutralizing this church so that it has no influence for good or for the One you serve. This place will end up being as dead as you have become," stated the vile spirit.

"I may be dead to this life, but I am alive to the One who possesses all power – all truth – and all life. Before the Holy One you cannot stand," announced Rasmus boldly.

"The people here are nearly dead spiritually. This place is more like a cemetery with only etched stone carvings serving as reminder of its inglorious past. I will finish them off.

Languish and die, this church will. It will cause us no interference anymore," asserted the dark demon.

"You are wrong, spirit. You have no right to be here and no power over a Holy Spirit filled church. God's Spirit will be invited to return, and God will be welcomed and celebrated here once more. God's presence will again fill this place," declared Rasmus triumphantly.

"That's a laugh," cackled the evil entity. "You and your God are a complete joke. What is even more humorous to me is the confidence you place in these pathetic people to return and express faith after this marvelous pandemic has swept like a reaper's scythe throughout this world. They have discovered that they do not need your impotent belief system. It has become useless to them. They have better things to do with their time."

At this, the demonic presence began to enlarge itself. It grew taller and took on an immense size, casting its dark shadow over much of the belfry. It hovered eerily and menacingly above Rasmus. It appeared that it wanted to reach out and consume him but for an irresistible barrier afforded to him by heaven.

"A quickened Spirit both holy and within the hearts of God's people can and will defeat you," shouted Rasmus.

Then pointing his ghostly index finger at his adversary hanging above him he said, "I command you, dark spirit in the precious name of Jesus, and through the blood Christ shed on the cross to heal his own and to defeat his enemies, depart from my presence and leave this belfry. Bother me no more here in this place! Away with you!"

Enunciating many grunts and groans of dissatisfaction, the visible essence of the wicked character appeared to be sucked through the floorboards of the belfry as if being consumed like cobwebs by a vacuum cleaner. This hasty departure to the expanse below cleared the belfry and left Rasmus victoriously and joyfully alone. He felt, however, that he was not at all a solitary figure on this stage of endeavor, for he believed he could hear the cheers coming from spectators in heaven rooting him on in his immortal combat. A feeling of peace settled in on this part of the church. Due to the outcome of the contest a feeling of satisfaction and accomplishment also grew within his essence. Emboldened by the righteousness of his cause and knowing that he was fortified by a company of spiritual allies, Rasmus felt great confidence in the conflict to fully dispatch his adversary.

In the moments following this confrontation a rather bizarre but alarming thought passed through Rasmus' mind. Could this foul entity have any kind of connection with the wife of the church's benefactor who lay in the little mausoleum off the sanctuary? "How could it," Rasmus thought to himself. What he had learned of the lady and her life was one of great virtue. She was highly regarded for her faith, morals, and ethics. The only connection that he could imagine in this regard is how evil enjoys twisting the fine and virtuous into expressions which accentuate everything foul and dark.

Such thoughts stimulated another notion upon which he contemplated. This season, and particularly the feast day of Saint Thomas, aligned with the winter solstice – the darkest time of the year. Was the coming of this evil upon him and the church at this time purposeful? Was it meant to deliver a message countering the Christ? Was this an attempt to diminish Christ's light in the hearts and minds of the congregants and perhaps to extinguish it forever? Rasmus could not be certain of this particular occurrence during this season, but he thought it very suspicious. Evil takes any opportunity to twist and turn that which is good and true and wholesome into something wicked and depraved and spoiled. Evil will employ any object, idea, or fine expression and corrupt it thoroughly if it possibly can. These thoughts and others passed through Rasmus' conscious deliberation of the current situation.

Rasmus was not the only being to encounter this dark lady on this particular day. The evil specter's purpose was to discourage and make uncomfortable anyone present in the church, especially the sanctuary. This included the church staff.

Jimmy Mack was a young man twenty-one years of age serving under the Junior Warden as part of the custodial staff. On the morning of the 22nd he was cleaning in the sanctuary when he came and asked Father Dave if he could talk with him.

Entering the church office, he first encountered the church secretary and receptionist – the delightful Francesca Regina Cristina. Francesca had only been in the employ of Holy Trinity Church for a brief period of time. She was a beautiful twenty-three-year-old young lady with long black hair and an olive complexion. Ethnically, she was Tuscan and Sicilian. She was bright and her face beamed when she smiled. Francesca was college educated with a degree in business and economics. She came to the Pittsburgh area seeking a position in her field. Her initial hopes of gainful employment were dashed by the expanding pandemic. She took the church job by necessity until she could arrange a more lucrative position. Much to her surprise, she discovered that she enjoyed this job immensely. Instantly, it seemed, she and Father Freeman developed not only a good collegial working relationship, but they came to like and enjoy each other tremendously. Their budding friendship became a little more complicated for Francesca as she began to develop affectionate feelings for the handsome young priest. She kept this to herself as she became Father Freeman's chief confidante in the church. She was most loyal to him and he came to trust her completely. In terms of her job, she possessed wonderful skills and people came to love her through her magnetic personality and cheerful countenance.

On this particular day Jimmy Mack, who was sweet on Francesca, stuck his head through the office door and said, "Whoa, Francesca, how ya doin' today?"

Jimmy Mack would do almost anything and find any excuse to stop by and converse with Francesca for a moment or two.

"I am doing just fine! And you?" replied the young lady sitting behind her desk.

"I was fine until a few moments ago when I seen this black object floatin' around the sanctuary," remarked Jimmy. "Is Father Dave in his office? I needs to talk wif him!"

"Yes, he is. Let me announce you and see if he is available to see you right now," Francesca said quickly.

"Before ya do that, I was wondering if after work you might want to get some eats wif me at the shop dahn the street? They makes the best soap and bread in town," nervously remarked the young man.

"Soup, Jimmy, you mean soup," corrected Francesca.

"Ya, that's right – soup," reiterated the now red-faced custodian. "Well, if ya don't want soup and a chipped chopped ham sammich maybe ya might want to watch the next Stiller game wif me dahn at the local tavern on Main Street. Since too, yer new to the area, we coulds go dahntahn n'at. I coulds show ya the sites – the fahntain, Mount Washington – wanna take the incline wif me – have ya been on either of the inclines yet?"

"I'd love to Jimmy, but I already have plans and I do not particularly enjoy watching football, even the Steelers." stated Francesca frankly. "I have already visited the sites you mentioned, and as for the soup and sandwich, your invitation is a nice one, but I cannot accept it. I'm sorry, but Jimmy you're trying too hard. I am not going to go out with you. You are a little too young for me. Now, let me please check on Father David for you."

"Too young, yer only two years or sumthin like that older'n me," replied Jimmy.

"Jimmy, I am not going to start the practice of being a 'cougar'!" Francesca smartly replied.

"That's not what a 'cougar' is," asserted Jimmy.

"Well, if I go out with you it would be like me starting to be one," Francesca shot back. "Jimmy, forget it, I am not going to go out with you – just forget it – nothing is going to happen between you and me so you might as well give up!"

Francesca knocked on Father Dave's office door and received permission to enter. She indicated to him that Jimmy Mack wanted to talk with him. Upon leaving Father Dave's office, Francesca said, "Ok Jimmy, he will see you now."

"Yello, Fodder Dave – how ya doin' today?" asked Jimmy.

"Come on in Jimmy. What can I do for you?" asked the good rector.

"Ya never told me that we have visitors here!" stated the young man.

"Don't tell me that you saw another rat. We just had the exterminators here!" cried Father Dave.

"Heck no," started Jimmy as he begun to spin his tale. "I was pushin' my buggy of cleanin' supplies an' stuff to reddup the sanctuary when some people entered the vestibule and into the narthex. They was lookin' arahnd an' seemed very curious and confused so I said, 'Yinz want sumthin?' They told me they was lookin' at the architecture and if it was ok if they walked arahnd for a while. I said 'sure', but tolds them I had work that needs done an' had to run the sweeper. They seemed very nebby – lookin' at everything. Then all a sudden, they runs ahta the church licky split. I had no idea why an' then thought that they might be stillin' sumthin. I ran after them but stopped at the crick. There was no way I was goin' ta catch them as fast as they was runnin'. So, I went back into the sanctuary an' decided ta take a break. It was almost time for lunch. I got out my pop, a jumbo sammich an' n'at. As I was puttin' some Heinz on it this here black thing swooshed by me an' then headed for the ruff. I dumped my pop and my sammich flew up into the air with it goin' everywhere. It made the tile parts of the floor very slippy. I cleaned it up with the dish rags I had on the buggy that was goin' ta the kitchen. Now I have to worsh them. Was that a ghost I seen? Have you seen it?"

"No, I haven't," replied Father Dave, "but other people have expressed to me the sights and sounds of some strange happenings in this building. It is quite unsettling to me. Failing to experience it, I do not know what to make of it."

Going on, Jimmy continued, "I said, 'Whoa dude, what is that?' It was like a black veil blowin' arahnd an' arahnd the place. It lasted fer a minute or so and then just disappeared. I gots ta tell ya Father Dave, this place is starting to give me the creeps. No fake, Fodder Dave, this here church of yers is really give'n me the jitters. I just hopes I don't git a case of the shits out of it!

"Thanks for informing me," stated Father Dave frankly. "I'll keep my eyes open and my ears peeled."

"I'll tell ya what," Jimmy went on, "if someone is tryin' to pull sumthin on me, if I ever catch 'em I'll give 'em a real lickin'. If it is some sort of a ghost an' I catch it I'll do the same."

"Jimmy," stated Father Dave with a partial smile on his face, "if it is some sort of an apparition, you'll never catch it."

"From now on when I'm in the sanctuary, I'll grab the clicker and play some music or a video on the screens when I'm workin' in there," said Jimmy with determination.

With that, Jimmy left the rector's office. His face brightening when he spied Francesca once more.

"Scooch over in your chair an' I'll sit down and show ya this trick I learned with gumbands," advanced Jimmy.

"Jimmy, I have far too much work to do today to share in games and tricks with you." announced Francesca firmly. "Shouldn't you be getting back to work?"

"Yeh, I guess so," agreed Jimmy with evident disappointment in his speech. "How's come ya won't go out wif me? I could shows ya a good time – properly speaking of course."

"Jimmy I cannot fault you for your persistence, but you are not my type so please stop asking me out before I begin to get angry with you. Now please, go back to work."

Disappointed, but not completely undaunted, Jimmy returned to his labor.

Situations such as that described by Jimmy to Father Dave were not uncommon in Holy Trinity Church. It was not a place in which people desired to tarry. There was definitely something foreboding and uncomfortable about it and within it.

Father Dave ran his hand through the hair on his head as he sat down once more at his desk in his office. He was a rather young man boasting a full head of light brown hair which matched his brown eyes. A handsome fellow, he was of average height and also slender. He had practically the same build as Father Feynman. This was his first permanent charge, though he had worked to assist other rectors in other churches prior to the bishop's recommendation and his election to the position. He was still single and the young ladies of the town loved him. He liked to work with his hands and as a youth received some training as a mechanic at a service station. He enjoyed being around people and was a terrific conversationalist who was conversant on almost any subject. He had wonderful pastoral skills and was very knowledgeable when it came to understanding the Bible. Like Father Feynman before him, he had graduated from the Trinity School for Ministry in Ambridge, Pennsylvania. As a student, he excelled in class. He certainly was a gifted speaker and enjoyed both preaching and teaching. He was a rather down to earth type of fellow with an attractive personality. Father Freeman was indeed a quality choice to follow Father Feynman.

These repeated sightings of some strange phantasm, reported to him by several individuals, perplexed Father Dave. If they continued, he would certainly have to launch a deeper more thorough investigation. He reasoned that he might even have to call in some professional help if he concluded that these unsettling circumstances derived from a devious source.

Perplexed, he called Francesca into his office. "Francesca, have you seen anything unusual in the sanctuary or around the church lately?" inquired Father Dave.

"No, I personally have not, but a few people have shared with me some strange occurrences recently." replied Francesca.

"Exactly what are they sharing with you?" pursued Father Dave.

"Well, they have informed me of hearing whispers in and around the sanctuary as well as seeing the movement of strange shadows in the nave and in the hallways," stated Francesca.

"If you encounter anything, please let me know." stated Father Dave. "Just in case, please be careful, until we figure out what is going on here. I wouldn't want something to frighten you or hurt you in any way. OK?"

"Yes, I will inform you directly and thank you for caring," responded Francesca. With this she paused at the door and stared at Father Dave with a look of adoration on her face.

"Thank you, Francesca. Right now I have to get back and concentrate on the holiday tasks immediately before me," he replied with a smile on his face.

He had to be honest with himself. He too was developing feelings for his secretary, but he was uncertain if he should allow these feelings to continue to grow and manifest themselves. If he did so, he was uncertain how to proceed. He had to think of the church, how it might look, what people might say, and what impact it could have on his career. This was especially true due to his thoughts about leaving the position soon after the holidays were over.

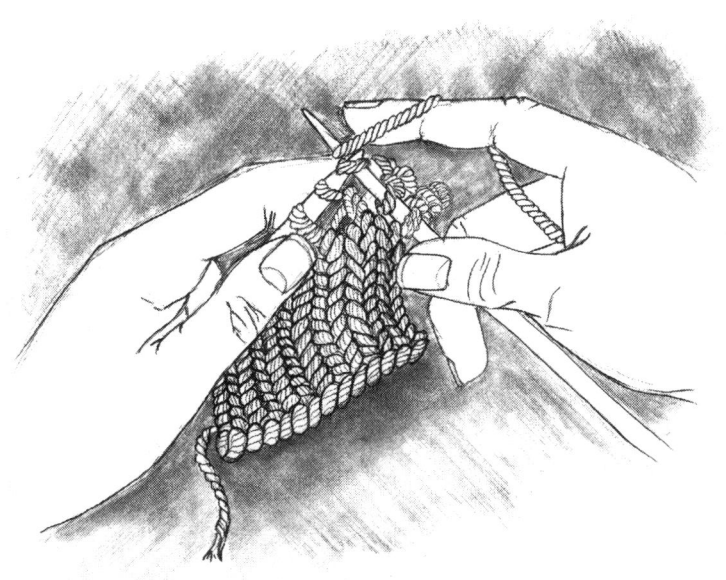

Stave 6
The Second Visit

elcoming the morning of the 22ⁿᵈ, Rasmus mentally prepared for his afternoon encounter with Margaret Jackman. Margaret was a woman he thoroughly enjoyed during his years at the parish. She had loved him as if he were one of her own. He conceived of her as a grandmotherly figure who cared for him deeply and gave him valuable and timely counsel. Margaret was a well-to-do widow who possessed a heart of gold. In spite of her wealth, she lived a life without pretense. She was humble. She never put on airs. Her desire in life was not to enrich herself, but to use her wealth to bless others. As quickly as she gave away her riches, her investments always replenished what she bequeathed to others.

At the same time, this aged woman worked with her hands, tirelessly knitting and sewing to aid the poor and needy. She also made clothing for the newborn babies in town. In this she was highly favored by the town folk. To many people in the village, she was like the biblical character in the ninth chapter of the book of Acts known as Tabitha, whose name was translated as Dorcas. Dorcas was a seamstress who made robes and clothing. Many people noted this parallel between the woman in Luke's second account and the town's dear benefactor.

Margaret's late husband became a famous businessman who served both his country and the communities of Western Pennsylvania well. He was greatly respected and garnered a great deal of praise and wealth during his career. He was a man of much integrity and responsibility. He made a lot of money, and being financially astute, invested quite well. Margaret was college educated and highly intelligent, but her primary calling in life had been to serve as a wife and mother. Like Helen Greenfield, her youth had slipped away from her as it does for us all. Unlike Helen, she had a vast reservoir of energy. For most of her life she had been quite active in the affairs of her community, professional associations, and church. She was a warm individual who possessed a disarming smile. Her laughter was contagious. In fact, she shook all over when she laughed. She would have made a quality stand in for Mrs. Claus. When she spoke, her face shined and her eyes communicated much attention to the subject at hand. She was a marvelous communicator and thoroughly enjoyed the company of others. Possessing a welcoming personality, she was a terrific hostess. She made everyone feel at ease in her presence. Her gray hair and slumping stature masked the youthful and spontaneous nature of her soul. Like so many individuals in his former parish, Rasmus came to adore her.

Margaret, who was still very vital and healthy in her ripe old age, unfortunately had become depressed and began to imagine herself as one isolated from others. "To what purpose is life?" she repeatedly asked herself in a pleading prayerful manner. Her husband was deceased. Her family was gone. Her many friends had either died or relocated. In her desire to be translated to the great beyond, her service faltered and she ceased attending fellowship events including worship. During this, her 89th year, she was searching for meaning, personal value, and purpose. All this had been made worse by the demise of her dear pastor friend whom she had frequently entertained for lunch. In her mind, he was irreplaceable.

Rasmus entered her house and approached her at the time he frequently visited, the noon hour. Margaret was in her usual seat at table, sipping chicken noodle soup and drinking hot tea. Rasmus took his time looking around her combination living and dining room. Once well decorated for the season, this year's garnishments were spartan. Only a few gifts were wrapped and stacked near the fireplace. There was no tree. It was a most humble setting for a multi-millionaire.

Rasmus did not want to startle her by parading in and making a grand entrance. He began to slowly take on visibility by emanating a small light as his countenance expanded. He shined the light onto the table where she sat in order to draw her attention. The light was not a shock to her constitution. It was, however, Rasmus' voice that proceeded from it that caused her to draw back in her seat with a sudden dread.

"Margaret, fear not!" stated Rasmus with a loving expression to his voice.

"It's Rasmus," he continued. "I have returned from heaven to visit you for a while. Oh, the joyous fellowship and conversation we shared so many times here in this room and at this very table. Please may I join you?"

"What are you? What do you want of me? Are you really there or is this some fanciful whimsy of the mind?" she asked.

"It is really and truly me, your rector and dear friend Rasmus," he quickly asserted. "I have come back to share in a brief time of fellowship and glad conversation with you again – like old times - as permitted by our gracious Majesty."

Margaret protested, "How can this be? How is it, that if it is truly you – you have come back to me? I was taught that God did not permit this sort of thing. I want to be joyful again in your presence – if it is truly your presence! And if it is true, then why? Why have you come to me? I know that I am not dreaming. I am fully awake and in complete charge of my faculties. How can this be real and not a flight of fancy conjured up by my mind?"

"Margaret, please allow me to explain," implored Rasmus as he took his customary seat at table. "I have been sent to encourage you, to reaffirm your value and service to our Lord, and to ask you for your assistance. I bring to you a divine assignment. I know that you have been pondering your life and wondering why you are still alive. 'To what purpose?' you have entreated the Holy Spirit. I know your desire is to depart to be with your Lord and Savior. I know of your wish to share in glad reunion with all those who have gone before you. Your hour will come. It draws near. It is, however, not your time according to God's plan."

"My life feels useless to me. I am advanced in age. My mobility is beginning to find its limitations. What good am I to others now?" shared Margaret.

"Margaret," immediately replied Rasmus, "your life and your life's work are marvelous and it has certainly gained the notice and attention of our Lord and Master. Your unselfishness and devotion to Christ's cause will reap you a great reward. Much goodness awaits you because you have placed other people first in your life and have been of great service to them. You are a true steward of the King's people, property, and possessions! The thoughts of your mind, the kindness of your heart, the compassion of your spirit, and the works of your hands are known to many – not in the least unto God. The love you share redounds to others who do emulate you. People pattern themselves after you. They share your example. They desire in their own lives to be the person you are - to do the things you do and in the way you do them. You do have a great following. Look at the knitting you achieve and the clothing you have made. Your work has aided missionaries, brightened lives in homeless shelters, provided material blessing for women and children in compromised circumstances. You have made blankets for babies and children. You have made warm clothing, wraps, and head wear to combat the cold of a winter's night. You have manufactured much joy. Some people may know you not, but they do know the works of your hands. You have blessed multitudes. You have done the things Jesus would do! And you have loved people as Jesus loves them."

"You overstate matters, Rasmus," retorted Margaret as she bowed her head humbly toward the table.

"No, I do not!" exclaimed Rasmus, "Remember, I am privy to some heavenly things. You have lived humbly amid your great wealth. No one would know of your means save for your generosity. How many ministers is it with whom you have partnered? How great are the medical resources you have sent overseas? How many of the lonely have you comforted? How many of those who seek refuge have you provided shelter? You support local foodbanks and numerous parish and diocesan mission associations. You have provided great donations to the Church locally, nationally, and internationally.

"Look Margaret," Rasmus continued, "you are a glad personage and a welcoming hostess. You provide people with warmth, hope in the betterment of the human spirit through Christ, a wholesome countenance, and the expression of what Christian fellowship is meant to be in all its beauty, breadth, and depth. You are one remarkable person. You are the mighty woman of valor of Proverbs 31. I know that your husband is dead, and that all your children, grandchildren, and great grandchildren are spread to the four corners of the nation, but you still have life and breath. Your life still has meaning. You still have mission and purpose to perform for the Christ. Return to church. Return to your life of passion for all things godly. Continue to share Christ's goodness, love, mercy, and blessing. Spread the joy of your stewardship and servanthood as a faithful disciple of our Lord and Christ. Practice the apostleship of encouraging people through your person and mission; to grasp, adhere, and own our Savior."

"What you say may have some truth, Father Feynman," interrupted Margaret, "but things are so different since you have gone. The church is not the same – for me, and for many others. The place does not possess the same atmosphere any-more. There is something cold and lifeless there. Many others have felt it as I do."

"I want you — more than that, God wants you - to give Father Freeman a chance," replied Rasmus. "He is new to the parish and the village. His heart and mind are in the right place. More than that, his heart and mind are right with God. He is a true and loyal under-shepherd faithful to his charge. Bless him by supporting him. Help him rein-fuse the church with joy and the might of Christian delight. Encourage others — talk to others — rally God's people to re-turn to Holy Trinity. This church is their spiritual home. A homecoming by God's people is long overdue. Start by being there on Christmas Eve. Talk it up and get the membership to pledge to come to services that night. Become a mighty force to cast out the shadows and provide light amid the darkness of despair and the woes of this world. I hope you will do so. In fact, I pray that you will. God needs your help in this effort to replace the foreboding and cold atmosphere that has invaded the church. Replace it with one of uplifted countenance and joy. Raise the roof on Christmas Eve by celebrating in praise and adoration the one who authored and finished our salvation. Will you? Will you please? Do it not for me. Do it not for Father Freeman. Do it not even for yourself. Do it for our blessed Savior and God's precious Holy Spirit. To God be the glory!

"It is time for me to depart now, Margaret," said Rasmus with a sad tone to his voice, "I will see you again, but not in this form or in this place. Thank you for all the glad times and good memories we shared. In God's time we will share many more good times and make many more glad memories.

The time is coming when there will be no more separation. The day draws nigh when we will not know the meaning of the word, 'end'."

With this final statement, Rasmus vanished suddenly. Gone right before her eyes, Margaret could not deny the experience of this visitation. Nor could she deny the things she felt as she conversed with her long, lost friend. Now was the time for reflection. It was now time for gathering her thoughts in the wake of what had just transpired, and with what she had been informed.

Stave 7

ᏚᎻe Ꮢhird Ᏼisit

The visit Rasmus shared with Margaret Jackman caused him to rejoice and to wonder to himself if she would pick up the challenge and follow through with a meaningful response. Rasmus spent the rest of the day reflecting on the biblical characters named Barnabas, Elijah, and Hezekiah. Barnabas was the nickname of a man whose given identity was Joseph. He was an important figure in the book of Acts. Barnabas meant, "son of encouragement." Luke says of him that "he was a good man...." Margaret was a good woman. She, like Barnabas, was "full of the Holy Spirit and faith, and brought many people to the Lord." "If one is full of the Spirit," reflected Rasmus, "how could she fail?" Rasmus noted that Elijah suffered from severe depression. On one occasion he wanted to die. God, in a dramatic demonstration of God's power and sovereignty, radically changed his thinking and provided the necessary reinforcement to conduct ministry for the remainder of his life. "God could do the same for Margaret," thought Rasmus. Hezekiah was not perfect, but he was given a life extension by God to accomplish much in Judah. God could provide Margaret, along with the others he was visiting, with an extension of life and the quality of health necessary to change the direction of things at Holy Trinity. It was now completely out of Rasmus' hands and up to God's Spirit. "God will come through," reasoned Rasmus.

Rasmus enjoyed the rest of the day and evening of the 22nd taking in the sights and sounds of his former habitation. Mentally, he prepared himself for his next visit to a man he highly respected named Edward Garland.

In his contemplation of his visits this day, he noted that all four of the individuals that heaven assigned to him were senior citizens. Each individual in one way or another was a leader in Holy Trinity Church. Many among Rasmus' extended family were Presbyterians. He knew the emphasis Presbyterian documents placed on leadership by the wisest, most faithful, and most dedicated individuals in a congregation. In reality, these were the type of people, save one, that he had been called to visit. The other visit was primarily, he believed, one of reclamation of a zealous but wayward soul.

Edward Garland was an optimistic, intelligent, accomplished, and creative individual who was gifted with organizational and administrative skills. He was talented at recognizing the gifts and interests of people and getting them into areas where they could excel. Edward had held the very high and responsible position as the chief executive officer in the employ of the manufacturing and research company for which he formerly labored. He was sharp intellectually and possessed a remarkable wit. His skills of analysis and synthesis also were part of his skill set. His face beamed when he smiled and his verbal expressions and tone put people at ease. He was a terrific listener and very adept at sharing constructive advice, while at the same time, being somewhat of an empath. He and his lovely wife were very social people who enjoyed song and dance, but they were also highly moral and ethical, valuing the more noble characteristics of humanity in this life. Edward, who retired young, possessed what seemed to be a reservoir of unbridled energy that needed to find expression. He utilized his talents in retirement focused on church and community. Edward was to begin to work closely with Father Feynman to revolutionize the ministry of Holy Trinity. With Rasmus' death, everything they had planned and were about to exercise in real time came to a grinding halt. Their partnership would never be. The positive and meaningful outcomes of their labor would never come to fruition. Edward never acknowledged it to others, but he felt that the Lord had let him down!

During the year that had passed, Edward had fallen ill. His illness was serious and might even be considered terminal. Recuperating from surgery, he would be discharged from the hospital on this "Eve of the Eve" as the 23rd of December is known to some. Edward was feeling well and very energetic. He was ready to go home and return to his lifestyle. It was morning when Rasmus arrived at Edward's hospital room. It was a private room filled with cheer: flowers, cards, a small

Christmas tree with colorful miniature lights and baubles, and a fistful of balloons carefully tied floating in the air.

Rasmus came right through the open door wearing the white attire of a member of the hospital staff. He wanted to have the look of a professional to camouflage his visit.

"Hi there Edward, how is it with you this day?" Rasmus cheerfully exclaimed.

"I am feeling just fine, thank you. In fact, I hope that you will now release me from your institution." retorted Edward. "I don't recognize you, doctor, though there is something familiar about you! Have we met previously?"

"Yes, we have, my good man. I am not a physician of the flesh. Let's just say that I am a physician of the soul and spirit." replied Rasmus.

"I must comment that your appearance is a bit ethereal. Your countenance portrays moments of transparency. Who are you? What are you? And why have you come to me?" cried Edward.

"It's me, Edward. It's Rasmus, your former rector," stated Rasmus almost in a whisper. "Do not be alarmed. I bring you no harm. You have nothing to fear from me. I who am dead to this life have been sent to you to request your assistance in a heavenly pursuit. I am on assignment from our great and glorious Majesty for the purpose of enlisting your help in the bestowal of a divine blessing on Holy Trinity Church and the town of Saxonburg."

Edward responded, "Rasmus, how do I know if you are really you?"

"It truly is me," retorted Rasmus. "Remember how we planned the future direction of the parish together? You, who were recently retired, offered your services to conduct much of the administration of the church to release my energies and time for a greater focus on ministry and mission. We discussed your idea two days prior to Saint Thomas' Day, two years and two days ago, at the corner coffee house. We had it all planned. Then I died to this life in what appeared to be a terrible accident and our plans came to naught. Without me, there was no way you could advance our proposed initiative. Since then, you have pulled back from working in the parish as trouble and much consternation among the membership have gripped the church. Too much argumentation has taken place in the light of my death and this has discouraged you. Do you believe that the one standing before you now, albeit in some mysterious spirit form, is your dear Rasmus?"

"What a strange occurrence this truly is!" Edward said in a loud voice. "No one would believe this unless they witnessed it for themselves. In some fantastic way I believe you ARE the ghost of my dear Father Feynman. Yes, I believe you have come to pay me a visit. Yes, I believe, phantom, that God has sent you to me for some important reason. You spark my curiosity. But before you grant me explanation, please tell me why you referred to your terrible fall in the way you did? What did you mean that your death had the appearance of an accident? Did someone cause you to plunge from up above? Were you murdered? Tell me, please!"

"In a way, my life was taken from me by another," answered Rasmus. "You might call it a murder. At least it is a murder of sorts. That is partially why I have been sent to you. I was assaulted by a demonic entity from the very pit of hell. In my attempt to escape from her, I lost my bearings and stepped back through the open floor above the altar."

"You refer to the entity as 'her'. Is this spirit that of a woman?" queried Edward.

"The entity appeared before me in the form of a little girl and then transformed into that of a grotesque female personage. I call this spirit the 'Lady of the Church,'" boldly asserted Rasmus. "This thing – this it – is no sweet woman. It is not even a former human in ghostly form as I am. This thing has been sent to discourage and destroy our beloved community of faith. I need your help to rid it from the premises! Can I trust in you to aid and assist me in this effort?"

Edward hesitated in his response, "Yes, I guess you can, but what can I do against such a power and an evil force? I have no gift of discernment and do not know the art of spiritual warfare."

"Leave that to me," Rasmus responded with confidence. "If you do as I instruct you, it will aid the situation immensely. Before I inform you how you can help get rid of this spiritual foe, there are two more things I must share with you. One is to ask you to perform another task. The other is to grant you a great blessing. First, let me take up my second request of you this morning. I ask you to return to our original idea. This time I need you to agree to pursue our concept of ministry with Father Freeman. Please honor me and keep alive my memory by assisting the parish's new priest. Father Freeman is a godly soul who loves the Lord dearly. He needs your help with this congregation. The church is so divided and many people have drifted away during the pandemic, as you well know. Go to him. Offer your services to him. Share our plan with him. I believe he will be open to your ideas and embrace them wholeheartedly. He would welcome the help, I am sure."

"I am sorry, Rasmus," stated Edward apologetically, "but my critique of the church and its people have soured in the two years since your death. In the first place, many individuals have devalued God's Word. I am afraid that a lot of people have become gods unto themselves. They have substituted their own thoughts and feelings for the Holy Writ. They have become their own final authority on all matters great and small. Secondly, the God they say they honor is one many believe is here to serve them, rather than the other way around. Today it is all about what God can do for you and your life instead of what one can do to serve and glorify God. I am afraid that the faith of many has become very self-oriented and egocentric. Thirdly, when it comes to serving in the church these days, people are very reluctant to volunteer." With these words, Edward became both agitated and passionate saying, "When they do volunteer, they want their task to be simple and short – easy and over with – just enough to feel good fooling themselves into thinking they have accomplished something significant. 'Forget any long-term commitment these days, no sir – not for me – too inhibiting upon those other pursuits in my life I value!' You can almost hear them say that, Rasmus. In fact, if they will not admit to saying exactly what I have just expressed, this it is precisely what they are thinking. I also find that those who do very little are the biggest critics of the labor others attempt to perform. They will offer many excuses for their own lack of participation. But woe to those who fail to do what the critics think should be done and the way in which they think it should be accomplished. Rasmus, I do not know if I want to place a target on myself." Pausing for a moment to reflect, Edward continued speaking slowly and deliberately, "On the other hand, are we not called to discomfort ourselves and take up that which is difficult? The thing I appreciate about God's calling is that we are given license to try. In our attempt to serve God, failure is permitted. What counts is that we are found involved in God's work. What is meaningful to God is doing the things God desires us to do to the best of our abilities, as poor as they may be. That's where God's grace becomes something very special indeed! Do you really believe, my friend, that what you have spoken to me is God's call upon my life at this time?"

"I do, Edward. I know so," replied Rasmus quite frankly.

"Yes, Rasmus, I will consider doing so, but one caveat is my declining health," responded Edward sadly. "I have been visited with news that causes me, my wife, and my family much sorrow."

"Say no more," interrupted Rasmus. "This is the blessing of which I spoke. Your God and my God knows of your plight. He is willing to give you a much longer life. You will be blessed with restored health. This dread illness will be taken away from you. You will be freed from its ugly grip now and in the future. It will not cause your earthly demise. God will instead translate you gently in God's good time."

Weeping profusely at the news, Edward kept repeating the words "thank you" and "bless you!" During this entire time no one entered Edward's room and the two seemed oblivious to the sounds of the hospital around them.

"This is what I need you to do to rid the church of the evil entity and to provide an uplift for Father Freeman and all the faithful," asserted Rasmus. "Tomorrow night is Christmas Eve. Gather your dear wife, your children and grandchildren. Make them attend the evening service. Encourage friends and relatives to attend. Help fill the church with song and praise to God. Lift up your voice! Fill the sanctuary with Christmas joy! Such praise and thanksgiving and merriment and joyful cheer will make the church unfit for anything untoward. Will you attend? Will you bring many? Will you delight in the Lord with all your heart and soul and strength? Fill the church with praise to our Almighty Sovereign."

Changing his thought, Rasmus digressed to forward a personal expression dear to his heart. He said to Edward, "I really do wish that we could have worked together in this realm. It would have been a great honor for me to labor beside you. I believe that I would have learned much. We would have made a great team! You always have been, and always will be, a marvelous individual to me in whom I greatly respect and admire."

Rasmus then uttered his final words to Edward, "Now follow through with what I shared with you. Be there, in force, tomorrow night!"

With that said, Rasmus vanished before Edward's eyes, leaving him in an astonished, but exhilarating mood, pondering much.

While Rasmus and Edward each spent the remainder of the morning and much of the afternoon reflecting upon their visit, things were becoming most interesting at the church. It was approaching the 5 o'clock hour when the office closed and church employees headed home.

Francesca entered the good rector's office and asked, "Is there anything else I can do for you before I leave for the day."

"Thank you, Francesca, but there is nothing else you can help me with today. You have a pleasant evening and I will see you in the morning," replied Father Dave.

With that Francesca turned off the lights and shut the door to her office. Walking toward the sanctuary she was suddenly met by Jimmy.

"J'eet yet today," cried Jimmy with determination in his voice. "I noticed that you did not stop for lunch. Sumthin' botherin' ya? Want to get a bite wif me?"

"No Jimmy, I do have some things to think about. I am just going to sit in the sanctuary for a while and do some praying and meditating," stated Francesca slowly and thoughtfully.

"Get aht, ya into all that prayin' stuff?" queried Jimmy as if he were being put on by her.

"Jimmy, I grew up in a very religious family. Being quiet before the Lord is important to me. It helps me clear my mind and maybe I'll get some direction from the Holy Spirit," stated Francesca. "Once more, I do have some things I need to think about, so please excuse me."

"Alwright, but have a good night an' don't let the dark shadows an' any unholy spirits of this place git to ya," stated Jimmy as he proceeded to leave her be.

Francesca sat in the darkened sanctuary deep in contemplation of her growing adoration of Father Dave. She desired to share her growing feelings of love for him, but was anxious about his response. Furthermore, she did not want to be too forward. She knew that he had been quite kind and gracious to her throughout their few months of working together, but he had never inquired of her if she was involved with someone. He did not know of any romantic interests she currently had or did have in the past. She knew that Father Dave was single and had never expressed to her any interest in female companionship. He did seem, so she thought, to be quite keen on her, considering his actions and statements to her. He seemed truly interested in her welfare and was quick to compliment her. Always appropriate around her, he was a true gentleman. She also noted that he would gift her from time to time and he was always inquiring if he could do anything to help her. Francesca also noted that he always paid close attention to her when she talked and he had never violated anything said in confidence.

As she sat there pondering all these things, she became puzzled and then alarmed at a form beginning to take shape in the chancel area. It appeared to be hovering over the pulpit. In her vision it grew larger and larger. Suddenly a hideous face began to form. It was followed by an audible whisper quickly captured by her ears.

"Do not fool yourself. He will never love you. He will not be here long enough to love you," stated the darkened form. With that a quiet but menacing laughter commenced as the figure faded from Francesca's view.

Francesca stood up quickly and screamed at the top of her voice. Hearing the scream, Father Dave came sprinting out of his office and into the sanctuary. There he spied a figure frozen in place and sobbing uncontrollably. To his surprise, it was Francesca. He immediately rushed to her side and threw his arms around her, holding her tight. She grabbed onto him and tried to form words through her sobs.

"What is wrong, Francesca? What happened? Why do I find you in such a condition? Please tell me! You are not hurt or anything?" rattled off Father Freeman.

Too frightened to talk, Francesca clung to him.

"Here, let's go into my office and you can tell me what happened," finally stated Father Dave.

Entering his office, Father Dave sat her down and then kneeled before her holding her arms in his hands. "Please tell me what this is all about. Why are you crying?"

Having difficulty forming words, Francesca finally said, "I-I-I s-s-saw it, Father Dave. It is b-b-big and d-d-dark and it spoke to me. It h-h-has the voice of a woman. It was f-f-floating in the air about the pulpit."

"What did it say to you?" Father Dave asked imploringly.

"I c-c-can't tell you, but it frightened me so", said Francesca as she began to find her voice and calm down. "This place is haunted. There is something in this building that I never want to see or hear again. Can you get rid of it, Father Dave? Can you make it go away?"

"I promise you, I will look into it immediately," stated the rector. "I can't have this thing scare the employees, frighten church members and visitors, and drive people away from this church. I promise you that I will attempt to get to the bottom of this. I know some people I can call who might be able to help us. I'll do that first thing in the morning. Please, tell me what it said to you."

"I can't", cried Francesca looking downward. "I just can't, please do not ask me anymore."

"You know you can trust me with anything, do you not?" pleaded Father Dave.

"Yes, I know I can trust you, but you have to trust me when I tell you I cannot tell you what it said," stated Francesca.

"OK, if you think differently about it, please tell me in the morning. It might help me understand what is going on around here," said Father Dave. "In the meantime, let me escort you home. I want to make sure you make it safe and sound. You are in no condition to drive. I'll drive you home and pick you up tomorrow morning. We'll just leave your car in the parking lot tonight."

"Thank you, Father Dave. You are probably right. I may not be in any condition to drive. I won't argue with you," agreed Francesca.

Francesca really appreciated the ride home. All night, however, her thoughts went back and forth over her frightening experience and the security of being held so close in Father David's arms. For his part, Father Dave was becoming more and more alarmed about the circumstances within his church. The thought that this could be demonic was something he did not want to contemplate, but apparently, he was now forced to do so. He was also troubled that the entity, if that is what it is, had frightened someone he secretly loved. He wondered if his rapidly growing feelings of love for Francesca were known to the entity. How could this be, he wondered, for he had never uttered any words of affection out loud either in public or in private? Did the entity have the ability to read his mind? What if he was unintentionally putting her at risk? If that were the case, his imminent departure following a disappointing season for the church might alleviate this situation and his alarm. Yet, saying farewell to Francesca was now something about which he shuddered to think. Could he really walk away from her? It was at this point that he came to realize that his feelings for her were genuine and inescapable. He had to admit to himself that he was deeply in love.

Stave 8

The Fourth and Final Visit

The evening was drawing late. For Rasmus, waiting in the church tower for the appointed time, there was one more visit to conduct. There was one more person to see. There was one more intrusion to make upon an individual's life. This one was deeply personal to Father Feynman. The individual had been a major thorn in his side during his ministry at Holy Trinity. She had spearheaded the opposition to his person, mission, and ministry. Gathering a following, she and her minions had made his time at the church more challenging and rather aggravating. Rasmus was not looking forward to this encounter. In his pent-up anger, this visit would actually take on more of the character of a haunting. Rasmus was determined not to hold back his pronouncements of disdain. He knew, however, that he had to be true to his mission in an attempt to change this individual's heart and behavior. Repentance was the order of the night. Forgiveness for the perpetrator who had caused him much grief during his life was also in play this evening. Dealing with this internal struggle, Rasmus repeatedly reviewed his approach and the numerous assertions he was about to make.

Agnes Hecate Heller was an appropriate name for this woman of slight stature. Agnes was a family name on her paternal side. It was a name passed down from generation to generation. Her mother was enamored with Greek mythology and gave her the middle name Hecate. Agnes did not particularly care for either of her appellations and referred to herself by the nickname "Ashes". As a child, she had the proclivity to wet her fingers and then dip them into her grandfather's cigar ash tray. Immediately her fingers would travel to her mouth where she would ingest the contents. Her doctors reasoned that this was due to some sort of iron deficiency. Regardless, a shortened version of the nickname "Ash" stuck.

Agnes was slender and had been quite attractive in her younger days. Throughout her adult life she strove hard to keep a youthful look - dying her hair, using all sorts of beauty products, and even subjecting herself to cosmetic surgery. She was popular growing up. She also attempted to be the center of attention. It was noted of her that she also spoke her mind. She was so outspoken at times that it became an intimidating factor for her in terms of friendship and dating.

Intelligent, witty, and communicative, she was a popular conversationalist. Gossip, however, became much her forte. Her eyesight had remained good all her life so that she only needed corrective lenses to read. She was found to be, despite her seventy-five years, still in relatively good health. Graduating near the top of her class, she always resented not being able to afford a college education. Widowed from a vigorous and hard-working husband several years earlier, Hecate secretly believed that she had married beneath her. She was never really proud of her husband who possessed immense mechanical skills. He was highly accomplished and well regarded by his employer, Alcoa – the Aluminum Company of America. In the community he was also known as a "fix-it" man. Many people brought various items to him for repair as he operated a tiny business on the side. He, and the lifestyle he offered her, never quite fit the status she envisioned for herself. She lamented that a professional man of means who was highly educated, well known in social circles, and commanded a large salary had eluded her. Following her husband's death, she began to live well beyond her means without his presence to control her spending habits. Agnes became over-extended financially and in debt. Her accumulated borrowing was used to finance her lifestyle in an attempt to portray to others a woman of means. Her indebtedness, if it did not cause a financial reckoning for her during what remained of her lifetime, would certainly be an issue for which her descendants, unhappily, would have to deal. She did not care. During her entire life she was primarily focused on herself. She took herself, her opinions, and her viewpoints quite seriously. She was unsympathetic, unforgiving, easily insulted, and an individual people actually feared due to her sharp tongue and her ability to get others to agree with her about almost anything. Once an individual fell out of favor with her, the person could anticipate from her nothing but derision.

A troubling circumstance began in her life not long after the death of Father Feynman. She began to hear whispers in the night as if someone were softly calling out to her. She not only heard these whispers in her head, but they were audible to her ear as well. This occurrence troubled her greatly. It did not happen every night, but was frequent enough to disturb her peace at eventide. It produced a great deal of fear and anxiety within her. The whisperer would say to her, "You know that you are right about things at the church. You are always right. People like yourself should have more of a voice in the affairs here. Your voice is one that needs to be heard. The rectors of the church have treated you poorly. They fear you and have robbed you of your rightful position and influence. They are jealous of you and your abilities. Join me and we'll make things right. Join me and we'll make this church our own."

Of course, this was the foul entity coming into her home and speaking to her in the darkness. What was even more disturbing was the suggestion of the whisperer to invite her into her person so that they could become one. This frightened Agnes more than anything else that she heard. She often wondered if she were losing her mind. A part of her desired to embrace the whisperer. She was tempted by the offer to wield real power in the church. Another part of her cautioned restraint due to the origin of the voice and also the outcome of such action. Sometimes Agnes felt that she was losing herself. In many ways she came to take pity on herself. She also began to distance herself from her contacts and social engagements. Her self-confidence was fading fast.

On the evening of the 23rd, the typical "Eve of the Eve" service that Father Feynman conducted annually had been removed by the Vestry. There would be no worship service this night.

Agnes was preparing to turn in for the night in her finely dressed cottage style house. Inside, her abode was a spectacle for guests, as the walls and shelving were full of many pictures and plaques. Also pictured were display after display of the honors and framed congratulatory letters and certificates she had accumulated during her lifetime.

Agnes turned down the bedding and donned her night clothing. She placed a cap over her flaming yellow hair. She entered the sitting room taking a glance at the dying fire in the hearth. Taking a seat near the fireplace, she prepared to drink a final hot toddy before entering her sleep. The libation, she believed, aided her slumber.

Suddenly, her night time musings were interrupted by a sharp banging on her front door. Before she could rise to answer, she heard the door open and then slam shut. Fearing that an intruder had entered her residence, she became paralyzed by fear. She sat petrified in her lounge chair; her eyes opened as wide as saucers. The next thing she heard was the clanging glass of her entranceway chandelier quaking violently. A ghastly sound, as if a boiler was letting off steam, also filled her house. There came one loud boom after another, which echoed from wall to wall, as the intruder took one deliberate step and then another. The creaking of the floor boards also indicated that the person who was violating her space was heading in her very direction. These perturbations were so different than what she had been experiencing with the whisperer. The thought that the whisperer was now coming to completely possess her, angry at her hesitation, shot through her brain. She was most terrified.

Feynman now entered her room right through the closed door. This door was meant not so much to keep out strangers, but to segregate warmth. Calling out her name, there was a hint of both terror and indignation to the sound of Rasmus' voice. As he moved slowly toward her, he began to manifest his phantom nature, visible, yet transparent.

Not knowing whether to attempt to take to flight or to grasp the fire iron near her to defend herself, Hecate remained glued to her chair. Hovering back and forth before her, Rasmus viewed her ominously as she had been the locus of the opposition he faced during his ministry. All the memories of her questioning every decision, deriding each and every event, gathering opposition to him among the membership, and being spurned by those she discipled flooded back to him, adding fuel to the fire that burned within his mind. If she did not fire the proverbial bullets at him, she certainly loved to make them for her loyalists to shoot. All this and more tumbled over and over again through Rasmus' reflections as if he were an actor in a horror movie.

Finally moved to speak, he slowly began his utterance. The volume of his voice, however, was very loud. "Good evening Agnes! Do you know who it is visiting you this fine night?"

"No, I do not," exclaimed Agnes in an obviously anxiety ridden voice.

"In life, I was your rector, Father Feynman. It was I you hassled, troubled, and spoke all manner of evil against," proclaimed the phantom.

"Why trouble me now?" cried Agnes. "Why come to me on this particular evening?"

"Am I here to speak retribution and pronounce judgement on you? Or am I here for some other purpose?" stated Ramus rhetorically, playing with her emotions and mind.

"Please do not proffer me with questions and your words of vengeance. Leave my presence at once. I will not abide your appearance or suffer your words this night or any night!" cried Agnes still visibly shaken while at that moment mustering every ounce of courage she possessed.

Extending her arm and hand, it appeared that she was reaching for the poking iron or some other object near the fireplace to hurl at the menacing phantasm which had breached her solitude. Stretching her arm as far as she could without looking in that direction, Rasmus spoke before she could grasp anything.

"There is nothing you can do to resist me. No tool or item will protect you from what I will say to you tonight. You will suffer my presence! You will listen to my words this evening!" Rasmus said with strength and conviction. "You did me much harm in life personally and ministerially. I wager that you were delighted with my sudden passing. I would not be surprised if you danced on my grave or sponsored a party with your admirers to celebrate my termination from the scene. Why were you so cruel? I ministered tenderly to you when your husband, God bless his dear soul, died. I comforted you when each of your good friends died as well. I became an advocate for you to take on public speaking roles and to sit on important boards and committees. I attempted to advance your interests. Yet you never failed to find some reason to put me down. You worked hard to change the opinion of many. You turned some against me. To what end I might ask? Tell me please, why all the animosity and hatred? Speak not! I already know. I'll tell you why. I'll proclaim the reasons which you think are hidden in the dark recesses of your soul!"

"Please, no more. Stop! Take your leave this very moment!" cried Agnes.

"I will not!", proclaimed Rasmus.

"You are a small and miserable woman who desired stature, influence, acclaim, recognition, and power," stated Rasmus with conviction. "You not only badgered me, but you went after some of my predecessors as well. Did you not? You pronounced boldly to Father Pete when he was elected to this charge, that he had to pass all decisions before you prior to approval by the Vestry. Father Andrew ended your employ in this parish when you challenged and spoke against him as well. When I came to Holy Trinity, I reached out to you and appealed to what I thought was your better character. Apparently, that was not enough. I have come to believe that you have no better person, nature, or character within your pathetic and miserable being. You never favored any rector save for the one who hired you to serve the church early in your life. Why was his stay so brief? Maybe he could not abide you as well. Whatever the reason, have you not taken it out on every priest since then? During my time at the church, I attempted much and accomplished more than any of my predecessors. Some things worked out quite well. Other things did not succeed as well as planned. Regardless of the success, the church was experiencing and the fine work we were doing in ministry and mission, you were always critical as if we were attempting nothing and doing less. Ministry is a complex web of highly visible components and iceberg responsibilities. There is much that you and others never perceived and about which you knew little. You pushed me down, as you pushed others down, in some vain attempt to elevate yourself. The luncheon meetings which you hosted at area taverns, tea rooms, and even in your own dining room, were pursued to employ your powers of persuasion to get people to agree with you and side with you about certain individuals and matters. To what good end or purpose was this? You have crippled the very church and mission of the Christ whose purpose you claim to espouse!"

"Please, please, no more," cried Agnes. "Is your purpose nothing more than a sentence of judgment and condemnation upon me?"

Responding quickly, Rasmus returned to the primary purpose for this haunting saying, "You are correct - enough of this! I am here to seek your reclamation and to give you one final opportunity to pursue redemption. The culture in which you now live have abandoned the biblical concepts of redemption, repentance, forgiveness, mercy, and grace. In this day, the thought that a person can rethink his or her position on certain matters in society and adjust or change opinions, thoughts, and actions appears to be no longer welcome. Public scrutiny renders a harsh and lasting judgment. Once pronounced, the scarlet letter pinned on you can never be erased or removed. This society knows nothing about forgiveness. If an individual or group violates what the new moral conscience considers to be sacred, one is forever guilty in their eyes. However, what is true of this culture and society is not true of God. Our God is a forgiving God. Our sin is not only erased, it is cast from our presence and put away forever. This opportunity for reclamation is for yourself and those you have influenced who abide by your dictates and declarations. Unless you do so, your award awaits you sooner than you may think. The new rector, Father Freeman needs nothing of your spite and callous disregard of persons.

Instead, the new rector needs your help. Holy Trinity Church needs your help. You can be a powerful influence for what is good, godly, gracious, and true. Your assistance is needed to turn the failing fortunes of this congregation into a powerful witness for the Christ and our heavenly Father. Your enthusiastic, positive, and optimistic support for the mission and ministry of the church can help produce a complete change in outlook and direction. It will also help to elevate your reputation from that of a constant critic, to one known as a faithful advocate of the good being generated and pouring forth from within the heart of this congregation. Your opposition will no longer be tolerated. Repent your attitude, words, and deeds. Redirect your energies. Fail to do so and what will change is your very address, and sooner than you may think. This I know for certain. God will not suffer you and your vile disputations any longer. Repent your sin and renew your righteous energies. Do so and the ponderous list of the grave disappointments and displeasures you have generated before the sight of the Almighty will be forgiven and covered over to be seen no more. Confess your evil. Embrace and own the ill attitudes and deeds you have concocted and spread abroad. Come to terms with it! Renounce it! Grasp it and cast it from your person! You are part of the foul presence in the midst of this church. Open a door to your heart and allow God to forgive you. Allow God to wash you clean in and through the holiness of God's precious Holy Spirt. Embrace the new person in Christ you can be. A person who will forever – for all time and eternity – be regarded as a blessed saint. This is what God desires for you. The choice is yours. God is ready to welcome and embrace you anew. God bids you to come. Will you reject such great mercy and magnanimous love?"

Speechless, but weeping quietly in her chair with her head bowed, Rasmus seemed to have struck a chord of both shame and sensibility within the thoroughly shattered consciousness of the woman. With this Rasmus continued, "Be in church tomorrow night for the Christmas Eve service. Make sure you speak to Father Freeman offering him your unconditional prayers and active support. Speak to those whose ear you have about your change of heart and mind. Enlist their support of time, treasure, and talent to assist Father Dave, and the outreach of the church. Speak not ill of anyone. Seek out only that which is good. Remember that Christian servanthood is not about the messenger, but the message. Remember to keep your eyes and mind fixed on God. Allow God to transform you into the person you know you need to be – the person I hope you secretly desire to be. You can do it. Even at your age you can be transformed and live a life that changes others."

"Please dear spirit, I need your help," revealed Agnes. "Sometimes at night I hear a voice. It is that of a female telling me to unite with her in some enterprise she has undertaken within the church. Thus far I have resisted, but I know not the derivation of this voice and what the consequences will be. I fear that I have entertained this whisperer much too long. What she says to me at times is tempting. I thought that you were the whisperer coming to get me when you first entered. Now I know that you are not. Can you please help me?"

"You are experiencing a foul and evil entity which portrays itself sometimes as a woman and at other times as a little child," replied Rasmus. "This is the source of much displeasure and consternation at the church. In fact, she is trying to take over the church and destroy it. Apparently, she wants to employ you to aid her foul designs. Do not join with her. Command her to leave your presence when she arrives. Do not listen to her. She will only cause you more harm and lead to further destruction in the church. I know that you would not desire that at all. You can help defeat her by following through with my previous suggestions. Resist her. Resist her completely. Do as Jesus' brother James informs us in his epistle; 'Submit yourself completely to God, resist the devil, and he will flee from you.' This is my best advice. It is time for you to make a decision. It is time for you to reclaim your true value in Holy Trinity Church. It is time for you to submit, resist, and unite with God's effort to do something remarkable with this church and its people."

"Spirits know no fatigue and never tire", so thought Rasmus. Yet, due to his passionate and imploring speech, he felt as if his energies were waning. "I will now take my leave and depart from your presence. You shall see me no more. I present to you the opportunity for a new life – a continuing life with real purpose and reason for being. It is either this or a withering termination of your person and influence. May your end, when it comes, be celebrated because of your faith and passion for righteousness. Do not allow yourself to end lonely and alone – your smallness evaporating into nothingness. Embrace your potential for goodness for the Lord's sake, and for the establishment of a magnificent eternal home."

"I also want you to know, dear Agnes," Rasmus stated slowly and compassionately, "that I forgive you for any evil you perpetrated against me while I was on earth. I will no longer hold onto any bitterness or resentment about you. I release you of this debt and burden. In so doing, I release myself of all my ill thoughts concerning our past history. I only desire the best for you now and in your coming eternity. I will love you as the sister in Christ regardless of your decision on the matters we have discussed here tonight."

Rasmus paused and then continued, "Once more, I bid you good night – a better night potentially in many ways than you have known your entire life. While you will no longer see or be visited by me, I, and all of heaven, will see and know your decision from this Eve of the Eve to the eventide of tomorrow. You have these hours to decide."

"Farewell spirit, and thank you," exclaimed Agnes in tears. "I will take seriously your words to me this night. Your words and visitation may yet provide me with great comfort. I will now reflect on them. Christmas time is a season to open one's heart anew to God as the apocalypse writer states in chapter 3 of his Revelation."

Interrupting, Rasmus repeated the verse, "'Here I am! I stand at the door and knock. If anyone hears my voice and opens the door, I will come in and eat with him, and he with me.' The next two verses go on to say, 'To the one who overcomes, I will give the right to sit with me on my throne, just as I overcame and sat down with my Father on his throne. He who has an ear, let him hear what the Spirit says to the churches.'"

"I may have opened the wrong door and to the wrong being. I will think mightily on this in your absence," stated Agnes frankly.

"You can also be," continued Rasmus, "one who overcomes. You can overcome your selfish inclinations, your temptation to cause others harm, the evil words and acts you perpetrate, and even the evil one and his representative who has been whispering to you."

Rasmus backed away and began to rise up in the air toward the ceiling. As he did so, his spirit slowly faded before her eyes until nothing of him remained in the sitting room with her.

Agnes, left tearful and perturbed, was both relieved at his departure and disquieted by the truth of his pronouncements. She knew the validity of that which he had spoken. She knew that what she experienced was a divine message meant not only for her reclamation, but for the good of many. It was all too real. It was a visitation that demanded an answer. The night would now be filled with the haunting thoughts of personal reflection, the thoughts of the evils she had perpetrated, and her need to conduct an acute re-evaluation of her life and person. It was time to rethink everything. And it was time to repent.

A
MOST JOYOUS
MERRY & MIGHTY
CHRISTMAS

Stave 9
Christmas Eve

As midnight came and "the Eve of the Eve" was no more, Feynman returned to the tower to pass the time. He was anxious to see if his visitations would bear any fruit. Had he convinced them to reconsider their positions and to get involved once more in the ministry and mission of Holy Trinity Church? Would some of them, maybe even all of them, join the effort to turn things around? He was cautious but hopeful about what might transpire later that new day.

Yes, he was hopeful, but he knew full well that the human soul often rejects suggestions of renewal and transformation. There are many human beings who do not believe that people can be reformed and change their attitudes, perspective, outlook, and behavior in life. Rasmus knew this to be true. His ministerial experience, however, witnessed to him that change – actual and complete change – can and often does occur. It happens more so if it is aided by divine influence. It is true that many people reject the promptings of the Spirit. Many people do choose the opposite of what the good Lord desires. Yet, Rasmus witnessed many who did repent of their past and renewed their allegiance to God. He also witnessed many who, for the first time in their lives, aligned themselves with the Almighty.

In occupying the tower through the night, Rasmus hoped that his continuing presence there would damper the influence of the vile lady resident in the nave, the transept, the chancel, the ambulatory and throughout all the areas within the church. This evil entity was constantly in motion. Its dark shadow swept at will through the building attempting to spread discouragement, disappointment, and an ill countenance upon anyone who entered this sanctuary. A disturber of both peace and prayer, this foul phantom sought to unsettle any and all who tried to find solace there. Feynman had been educated in the Christian rites for deliverance from evil spirits, but his authority in this case was limited. It would take the living who desired transformation to overthrow and run this vile presence out of their midst. This appeared to him to be God's will and *modus operandi* in terms of the divine sanction to be performed at Holy Trinity Church. Through their determination to light a new fire of godly dedication, devotion, worship, and praise in their communion, the darkness brought on by this foul entity could be vanquished.

Feynman hoped that the night would pass in a silent and tranquil way. What he experienced was anything but a "silent night." Rising up from the bowels of the church his ears began to pick up sounds that were both chilling and terrifying. The sound that was ascending to him was akin to that of a giant or some monstrous beast making thunder with each ponderous step it was taking. Surely, he thought, those outside must be able to hear what was odiously audible to his soul. Descending from his high perch, he flew into the great cavity of the nave. The booming echoes which reverberated from wall to wall and floor to ceiling and back again ceased. They were replaced by the almost imperceptible sound of a woman weeping. The crying slowly grew louder and louder. As it did its character began to transition into a desperate and uncontrollable sobbing. This was followed by shrieks and screams. This awful noise would suddenly cease only to be followed by a deafening silence. Then, in a startling way it would commence anew. As Rasmus hovered in the midst of the sanctuary, he noticed that a swirling sound with the distinct feel of rushing air was circulating around him. It continually picked up speed. The noise it made grew until it was nearly deafening. He could also see objects in the air flying about him. They were the substance of the church: chairs, pews, hymnbooks, chancel appointments, lesson papers, and finally building material. In his vision the church was self-destructing as if hit by a ferocious tornado. It was deconstructing from inside out. Then came the image of flames moving about him as in a great conflagration, consuming everything. All of this was, of course, an illusion created by the entity to deceive him into affirming its power to destroy and obliterate the place and everything for which it stood. Then suddenly came dead silence. Instead of the "gentle whisper" of Elijah's encounter with God, what followed next was a vociferous and raucous cacophony of diabolical assertions.

"You will not win over me, you pathetic and miserable piece of offal and effluvium!" shouted the demonic voice from each and every direction. "You are nothing. You have not fiber, sinew, or psyche. You are less than a trifle. You are chaff blown around by the wind. Your humanity is gone. You are not some angelic being or super saint. You have no power over me as you think. Your effort is picayune and trivial. You will not succeed against my magnificence and superlative dark power. You may have won a skirmish, but you will not win the battle for dominance in this theater."

Rasmus then returned her assertions. "You are correct oh evil one. I am less than a tiny insignificant speck in this whole glorious universe. I have no power of my own to defeat and dispatch you."

"This is my place," interrupted the entity. "I will own it. I will certainly secure it this season. Your exertion to expel me is both miniscule and pathetic. So, go back from where you came. You are not welcome here in my house. Be gone!"

Rasmus understood that the lady of the church was employing the language and methodology of the deliverance ministry in an attempt to purge him from the building rather than the other way around. In her twisted reasoning the wizardry of incantation and the pronouncement of spells might succeed with someone of dubious authority. His authority, however, came directly from the throne. The authority under which he operated was far more powerful than what she possessed from the fires of hell. This battle was not, however, just a conflict pitting power against power. It was also about truth and righteousness. Rasmus knew that both of these elements in the confrontation accentuated his abilities as gifted to him by Providence. God's veracity was always at stake in this cosmic war. God's Word meant everything to God. Truth and righteousness were precious to God. This whole engagement was not just about power. Power often proves nothing but who has the most might at a particular time and place. What counts to God is that God's veracity be understood as the ultimate Word in and beyond the universe. Rasmus was fighting for God's most precious quality and characteristic. This battle was more than just for Holy Trinity Church and its congregants. It was a struggle for understanding the very nature of a holy God.

"I will not leave this place, foul spirit," cried Rasmus defiantly. "How dare you try to turn and employ the language of spiritual strife against me. You will not be able to remain in the face of God's precious Holy Spirit. With the coming of this new day the issue will be decided between us. I leave it to Providence to work God's will resulting in your complete removal from this place. Disturb me no more this night."

With those words, Father Feynman removed himself to the belfry once more. The remainder of the night grew quiet. There he remained patiently awaiting the rising of the sun.

On this morning of the 24th he delighted in the colors and brilliance of the advancing orb upon this plot of earth he so loved. As the day progressed, he enjoyed viewing the preparations being made for the service. In particular, he was delighted with the ornamentation which now adorned the sanctuary and every corner of this large church. Decked out with much evergreen, decorative banners, colorful church appointments, multi-lighted Christmas trees, and the placement of scores of candelabra; the sanctuary portrayed a very festive atmosphere. Rasmus was sure people would be most delighted.

Now that the scourge of the pandemic was waning, this would be the first Christmas Eve in two years wherein people could congregate in relative comfort. A light snow began to fall over the village and countryside. It was not heavy enough to cause any difficulty in walking or to impede travel. It was just enough to add to an atmosphere of cheer to this delightful celebration.

Finally, the time drew nigh for the congregants to enter. The first one present was Father Dave himself. He arrived very early. He came several hours prior to the service. Rasmus watched as he sat on the chancel steps and bowed his head in prayer. He observed Father Dave lift his head and arms to heaven as if he were expecting to receive some blessing from above that he must catch in his limbs and cradle to his breast. Though Father Dave's expectations for the night were not great, yet in his anxious anticipation he affirmed the God who could bring great things to pass.

In time the organist and choir director entered the building. Members of the choir and musicians ingressed as well. The deaconate and those who had various responsibilities in the arrangements and conduct of the service arrived and found themselves busy making preparations so that everything was ready. Whispers, however, were evident as the early arrivals wondered just how vacant the sanctuary might be that night. It would be a pity to put forth such effort when few people would be present to appreciate the expenditure of their time and labor.

Rector Freeman positioned himself at the large double doors defining the space between the vestibule and the narthex. He had decided to greet all those who planned to worship and participate in this evening's service. People began to enter. He was pleasantly surprised at the number of early arrivals. He also noticed how cheerful and happy people appeared to be coming to worship this evening. There were many smiling faces and statements of glad expression uttered extending holiday tidings one to another. Among the early arrivals was Helen Greenfield.

Warmly greeting the rector Helen, possessing a new found zeal, began to speak, "Father Dave, I have come early to sit in the relative silence of the sanctuary to pray for you and tonight's service. It is my earnest prayer that God's precious Holy Spirit speaks to many a soul tonight." With a broad smile on her face she went on, "I have spent much time contemplating my purpose here in this congregation at this time in my life. I have decided to redouble my prayers for you and the church. I want to do whatever I can to help you. Please forward to me any prayer concerns you might have that I may petition God. I do pray that a sweet spirit fills the church this evening and that our praise to God becomes an acceptable offering to our Lord. I will now find a seat and begin my supplication." With that Helen was off to perform her stated intent.

Father Dave was elated! He felt a new warmth of spirit within his being. The church's prayer warrior had arrived and was now on duty. What joy this was to him as he considered it to be the first miracle of the evening.

Feynman was beside himself with joy as well as he stood invisible behind Freeman taking it all in! "This is a good start in order to dispatch the darkness," he thought to himself.

Soon after Helen entered and took her seat, Edward Garland and his entire entourage of family, friends, and relatives swelled the entrance way and soon the sanctuary.

Edward greeted Freeman with a hearty hello and a healthy double clasping of the hands. "Father Dave, I once formulated a plan to help the church and our dear late Father Rasmus, God bless his soul. I think it is time to dust it off and present it to you. I think I can help assist and aid your ministry and that of this fine church. Let's get together for some coffee and holiday delicacies and discuss it before the end of these twelve days. I think that together we can do something special here. I think we can help to make this place one of shalom pouring forth through these doors to the whole community. Glad tidings to you tonight. God bless you and your message to us. I am looking forward to what you have to share. Please find encouragement in what I have said to you. My family and I are with you and we will work alongside of you to promote this vital ministry. Tonight, Father,  do not hold back; preach the good news, share the advent of our Savior, proclaim the joy of this most astounding event in divine/human history. Father, make us very glad this evening – very glad indeed!"

At this Edward joined his family who had already entered the sanctuary and were presently taking their seats in the pews.

Freeman's joy on the evening had just doubled. He found renewed strength and personal confidence in what he had just experienced and what Edward had said to him.

Feynman was also elated. "So far tonight that's two for four," he mused to himself as his confidence in the possibility of going four for four, seemed to be much more of a possibility. Continuing to stand behind Freeman, he was delighted to see so many faces of the people he knew and loved so much while rector.

Margaret Jackman was the next of the four Rasmus visited to arrive. She went straight to Father Dave. Looking up at him she said, "Father Freeman, please forgive me for my lack of commitment to you and this glad fellowship. Here now, take this envelope," as she thrust it into his hand. "Inside, you will find three checks," she stated, now whispering. "A rather large one in support of the church. Another one in support of the church's mission fund. And a third one for the time-honored Boxing Day offering given to the poor. We still practice Boxing Day, do we not?"

"Yes, we do. We are one of very few Anglican churches who still participate in this ancient custom. I certainly thank you, Margaret" replied Father David somewhat taken back by her spontaneous generosity.

Margaret continued, "From now on I will support this church and its work in mission and in the community as I did when Father Feynman was here. Also, from now on I will once again attend worship on a regular basis. Please come and visit me when you can. I do want to talk with you concerning my continuing support of the Lord's work. I certainly pray that a river of blessing in the days to come will be poured out from this church, down our village streets, and out to the whole wide world. Tonight, may all of us make a joyful noise to the Lord for the coming of our Savior to abide with us. Let us 'raise the roof' as I have heard this expression spoken a number of times in my life!" With this Margaret chuckled and continued her steps toward the sanctuary.

Rasmus was more than delighted with Margaret's presence that evening. As he stood just out of the way, however, he was getting a bit nervous due to the absence, thus far, of Mrs. Heller. Would she appear? Would she make the evening complete?

People were pouring through the entranceway. When Father Dave spied Francesca coming through the doors a big smile grew on his face. He was most pleased to greet Francesca and her parents as they decided to attend the service that evening. Mr. and Mrs. Cristina had recently relocated to the area to live near their daughter. Along with them came other members of Francesca's family who were visiting the area for the holiday.

"I'll see you following the service," she told Father Dave. "I'll wait around until you have time to talk with me. I have something I want to share with you, that is, if you don't mind and if you don't have any other plans."

"That's fine, Francesca," he retorted. "I would enjoy talking with you, and I do not have any other plans for the evening after the service." Happy, but both anxious and inquisitive as to the substance of Francesca's desire to have a private conversation with him, Father Freeman altered the focus of the conversation. "It looks like it is going to be a very busy night for Holy Trinity. We might just pack the place!"

"I hope so for your sake," she said. "You work so hard. It would be really fantastic to have a full house tonight! From what I hear, it has been a long time!"

"Indeed, it has," responded Father Dave. "I have never experienced a full congregation. Please enjoy the service and I am happy that your family has accompanied you."

The rows of pews were quickly filling up. Father Freeman was joined by the choir, the acolytes, and the cross bearer preparing for the night's processional hymn. Rasmus, at that very moment, standing away from the people gathering near one of the church's giant columns, spied three very familiar people. It was his dear wife Laurel and their two children. Oh, the joy he felt as he invisibly moved closer to them. They looked healthy and happy. There was no hint of sadness or sorrow upon their smiling faces as people shared with them a hearty greeting. Rasmus overheard them say that they had returned to the town to share this night which had always been important to their dear Rasmus. They had made reservations at the town's hotel and would be staying through Christmas morning. Laurel indicated that it was important to her and the children to renew this part of the family's Christmas tradition. Laurel, John Gilbert, and Janet Isabella scurried to an empty portion of a pew near the back. The organ prelude was now transitioning into the first hymn as the congregation stood and the lengthy processional commenced.

As Father Freeman reached the chancel and climbed its steps, he turned from the altar and moved to the presider's chair near the Gospel Ambo. There he turned again and looked out over the congregation which was involved in enthusiastic singing. Suddenly, he spied Agnes Heller and a significant number of people making their own procession into the sanctuary. His emotions at this time were a mixture of both foreboding as to what she might be up to and wonderment at her presence. The late arrivals took up all the remaining seats in the sanctuary. Mrs. Heller herself came forward and sat in the very first pew. Father Dave hesitated and then looked at her. She made eye contact with him nodding her head approvingly. An affirming smile beamed across her face. Father Freeman in the ecstasy of his mind stated prayerfully, "This is truly a night of miracles after all!"

Rasmus was most delighted and ebullient as well. His mission had produced much fruit. It had turned out to be a finer evening than he actually thought was possible. And then he remembered Gabriel's statement to Mary that "with God all things are possible." His fear of only a middling outcome was now cast out.

Something to be cast out and eliminated which was more significant than his fear now drew his complete attention. The sanctuary was now full of people. More than that, however, it was full of light and raised voices praising God. People were expressing love to God, and through God to each other. Barriers between family members and neighbors who were estranged were also mellowing and melting away. The atmosphere of the church was becoming charged with the attributes of the Spirit: grace, peace, joy, love, faith, hope, and forgiveness. The possibility of personal transformation in many a heart and mind of the worshippers was taking place. It was becoming a glorious evening raising positive prospects for the future of the church and its membership. In their mirth on this night and in this season, the worshippers knew nothing of the spiritual battle that was taking place in their midst.

The lady of the church, that malevolent entity, was immersed in panic. Scurrying about to find a corner of the church in which to reside, she had to locate a cavity away from the light and the raised voices echoing throughout the building. This she discovered, much to her horror, was impossible to find. As the worshippers raised their voices in song and as the pipe organ and musicians played, the sound was one from which she could not escape. Just the thought of God was intolerable to her. As the Spirit of God grew in its manifestation in the church, she discovered her presence receding. Her power was fading fast. In moans and shrieks of which only Rasmus could hear, she became smaller and smaller until her being evaporated into nothingness and she was completely gone. The evil entity had, at last, been vanquished.

With uplifted countenance, the people praised the God of the incarnation and virgin birth. A new essence of salvation's splendor filled their hearts. This new fire of the Spirit burned brightly among the congregants and was reflected throughout the stone edifice. Praise to God reverberated from floor to ceiling and from wall to wall. Everywhere it could be heard in its magnificence. The church was now once more filled with the Holy Spirit. There was no longer room for any dark presence. They had invited God back into their fellowship. God was present again in the fullness of God's majesty and beauty. All of this was much to the immense delight of Rasmus. He had now witnessed the complete turn around of his former parish. He had now witnessed the beginning of a new effort to complete his long-held desires for his former church. It was for him a most joyous, merry, and mighty Christmas!

Stave 10
Christmas Day

ith the casting forth from the church of the evil
entity that fouled the atmosphere and depressed
God's faithful people within Holy Trinity Church, Rasmus
was most celebrative and ecstatic. His joy in the finality of
his assignment was almost complete. When you consider that
all four of his visitations to the living proved fruitful, that the
church had been set free from the evil entity that possessed it,
that Father Dave now had the opportunity to continue Rasmus' work, and most precious of all, he had located and been

in the presence of his dear family – there was little more that could be accomplished.

Rasmus accompanied his family, without their knowledge of course, back to their lodging. He delighted in listening to their conversation as they walked down the street to the inn. He hovered near them as they took to table and shared evening refreshments. He tarried with them as long as he thought it wise. When they gathered themselves to their room to turn in for the night, off he flew back to Holy Trinity to see how things fared post-service. He was delighted that he was apparently afforded this opportunity by heaven to tarry for a while and to experience some continuing time on earth.

It was now just past midnight. There in the subdued lighting of the sanctuary sat Father Dave on the chancel steps reflecting on his new found joy in prayers answered and lives changed. Praising and thanking the Lord in loud voice for the success of the evening, little did he know that Father Feynman had come to sit beside him, delighted as well in what had transpired.

Rasmus knew that he could not reveal himself to Father Freeman, but in the darkened nave he whispered his thoughts, "You have received a great gift from the Almighty, Father Dave. It is now up to you to do that which I was cut off from accomplishing. I wish for you Godspeed in the performance of your ministry. My hope and prayer for you is that you will take this church well beyond my own dreams and plans for this place and its people. God has indeed been good to both of us. Your prayers and my earnest yearnings have been answered and fulfilled this night. Make good on what God has done here this evening. Enjoy the blessing and magnify it in outreach to many. Have a mighty Christmas, Father Dave, and a fulfilling season of Epiphany as your ministry goes forward with new vitality, in a new light, and with a renewed purpose."

With that Rasmus made his departure. His spirit spiraled upward into the church tower to his haunt in the belfry. There he remained, anxiously awaiting dawn's early light and the hope of being permitted to see his family here on earth one last time.

Meanwhile, Francesca had departed with her family to enjoy some food and drink at The Village Tavern down the street. She re-entered the church just moments after Rasmus took his flight from the sanctuary. From the rear of the nave, she spied David sitting on the chancel steps. When he saw her his face lit up and he produced a big warm grin beaming from ear to ear. She took off her coat and began walking down the aisle toward him.

"Thank you for waiting for me. I knew I'd find you still here," she said. "I'm sorry if I kept you waiting, but my family was in a very merry mood this evening as I spent some time with them over at the tavern. They enjoyed the service. And you, well, you were wonderful tonight! Your message was fantastic and the whole service was so beautiful."

"Thank you, Francesca. I don't think I could do this work without your encouragement and support," he said to her tenderly. "You make my job so much easier and worthwhile. I really appreciate your work for the church, and in particular, what you do to help me. I know you have something you want to share with me, and I also have something I desire to share with you. So please, come and be seated beside me," as he patted the step upon which he sat.

Francesca, always beautiful, well-groomed, and immaculately dressed, was particularly stunning in her red dress this night. David couldn't get over how marvelous she looked. As she approached him, David stood up, took her hand in his, and invited her to sit down and share one of the risers leading up to the chancel with him. Up close now, Francesca looked absolutely amazing in the dim light of the sanctuary. Their eyes met and became fixed on each other. His gaze upon her communicated much love. Francesca sensed that and it increased her confidence in what she was about to say to him.

"David, I know that on Christmas Day you have no dining plans with your parents and siblings living so far away," she, with some anxiety, began. "I want you to dine with me and my family. We all would enjoy having you over to spend the day. Please come and share in our Christmas celebration and hospitality. You may arrive any time after 12 pm. We plan to dine at four. Please do not turn down our invitation."

"Well, that's great, Francesca, but only if you really want me to," remarked Father Dave in a coy way.

"Yes, well, I really like you, David," gently expressed Francesca. "I know you are my boss and I might be a bit out of line saying this, but I love spending time with you and being around you. You are a marvelous person. I hope you do not mind me saying that, but it's the truth."

At this a couple tears rolled down her blushing cheeks.

Hesitating, she went on, "Forgive me for saying this, but I have developed feelings for you." Francesca was now even more nervous as she began to tremble ever so slightly.

"Francesca, I have to be truthful with you," rapidly replied David with both a growing confidence and sporting a smile. "I too have developed feelings for you. In fact, I am growing in love with you. Yes, I want to spend Christmas Day with you, and my hope is that we will be able, if you desire, to spend many, many Christmas Days together in the future."

"I would love that," she said to him relieved and with a cheery glow upon her face.

The two of them drew near to each other. Their lips touched and their arms wrapped around each other in a full embrace. In all the drama of that Christmas Eve, something else was born that night – a love that would brightly glow throughout many years to come.

Morning came all too quickly. It was a bright and brisk Christmas morning. Beams of sunlight seemed to cause everything to sparkle. Rasmus vacated the tower before the annual ringing of the bell which took place on such holidays as this. He traveled to the inn and shared in the table fellowship of his family eating breakfast. Of course, he remained invisible and spoke not a word as much as he desired to do so.

During breakfast Laurel said to her children, "We have one more task today before we drive home and share in opening gifts and eating Christmas dinner with your grandparents. I have obtained a special wreath made of holly and ivy with bright red berries that we will place on your Father's grave. This will be a new family tradition for us. Each Christmas Eve we will return to Holy Trinity to share in the service. Every Christmas morning, we will visit your father's grave and honor his faithful love to us and to God."

Walking beside them to the town cemetery, Rasmus saw his grave for the first time. There on the stone was etched his

name and that of his dear wife. Underneath were the words from Revelation 21:5 "Behold, I make all things new!" How appropriate was this phrase to him! He now could testify to the truth of that declaration by the Almighty King. Laurel passed the wreath to John Gilbert who properly pinned its tines into the soil. The three of them all held each other as they paused for a couple of minutes looking at the grave in solemn silence.

Breaking the quiet, Laurel finally spoke. "Children, the best thing about Christmas is that God's love is never ending. You see, our God never gives up on us. God's desire is to embrace all of us forever and ever. The grave matters not, for God gives us eternity, and we must receive it and handle it with love. The greatest gift you can give anyone in imitation of God at Christmas, and throughout the year, is love. God loves your father. With God, he still is! We all miss you, dear," she said as she looked up into the sky.

Amid tears she continued, "We love you and hope in some way you can see us right now. Please know that we will never forget you. We hope that you will have a fine Christmas Day in Heaven. We will come here and visit you again, my love. Good bye, for now!"

At that moment Rasmus wrapped his soulish arms around his family. A divine wind suddenly swirled around them to which Laurel said, "Children, I get a real sense that your father's spirit is present with us this very moment. Tell him how much you love him!"

"We love you, Daddy," they said repeatedly.

"Well, children, we have much to do today - let us be off!" Laurel finally stated amid tears.

Rasmus watched them depart. He did not follow. Instead Rasmus tarried by his grave. He longingly looked at them moving away from him as Laurel closed the gate behind them. As she did so she glanced one more time at the grave and with a tearful smile on her face she whispered the words, "I'll catch you later!" Indeed, she would!

THE FREEMANS

Stave 11

ᗞhe Future Consummation of the ᗞale

As soon as Laurel and the children were out of his sight, Rasmus was immediately gathered again to heaven. Here he received from the heavenly host much praise and congratulatory greetings for the accomplishment of his mission. He heard these very words from the throne acknowledging his person and his earthly endeavors, "Well done good and faithful servant. You have been faithful in many things. Come now and share your master's happiness."

Father David Freeman went on to enjoy a long, meaningful, and highly successful ministry at Holy Trinity Church.

This occurred in both the way the world counts things and in the manner that heaven defines success. The affection that David and Francesca shared with each other following the Christmas Eve service blossomed and bloomed. David and Francesca were engaged by the summer. They were married during the Sunday 11 o'clock morning worship service at Holy Trinity Church. This occurred one fine day during the Advent season to the delight of all. Even Jimmy Mack, who developed other interests both relationally and professionally, was happy to witness the nuptials.

While Jimmy Mack always struggled with the King's English, he was not an idiot. Neither was he slothful. He was, in fact, an energetic, determined, and resourceful young man. He eventually opened and operated his own professional cleaning business with many people in his employ. Not only did he become successful, but he ended up being rather wealthy as well. Eventually uniting as a member of Holy Trinity Church, he always looked upon Francesca and David as his friends. He had many interesting stories to share with people concerning his experiences at the church, and he delighted to tell anyone who would listen.

Francesca continued to work as the church receptionist and secretary, both full time and then part time as she bore David children. The couple would have it no other way, as the two of them adored each other their entire lives. Their love and admiration for each other knew no bounds. Their lives became a testimony to the love between a husband and a wife in and through the person of Jesus Christ.

Helen Greenfield continued her vital prayer ministry for a few more years until God called her to her reward. She was faithful in prayer, attendance, and fellowship right up to the last day of her earthly life.

Margaret Jackman never questioned her purpose in life again. She continued her active stewardship in many fine ways. Her resources only kept growing as she kept sharing with the church and others. She died as she desired. She was taken quickly in one moment of time, without suffering any lingering illness.

Edward Garland worked alongside of Rector Freeman, liberating him from much of the administrative chores of the parish. Concentrating on ministry and mission, Father Dave was able to accomplish much. Edward Garland never did die from the illness that would have robbed him of his earthly life. When he passed from this life to the next, he did so quickly. When he died to this life he was surrounded by the presence and comforting words of his beloved family.

Agnes Heller was true to her transformation. A discouraging word never again passed her lips. She, and those who admired her, labored feverishly for the work of the Lord in Holy Trinity Parish. After a very long life of quality health, she too was translated to the company of the faithful.

It must be mentioned that Edward Garland and Margaret Jackman did one more very fine thing to magnify and honor the person and work of Father Feynman. They established a foundation in his name. They contributed generously to inaugurate the foundation. The foundation then contributed hefty sums of money to promote philanthropic work. They actively encouraged others to contribute as well. In this they were most successful. Laurel became the manager and chief executive officer of the foundation. Other than her children, grandchildren, and great grandchildren, it became the primary purpose of her life and service unto God. She poured herself into it. It must also be mentioned that she never remarried. Her heart, both in this life and in the next, belonged to Rasmus. Keeping their promise, each year the family would return to Saxonburg on Christmas Eve and attend the service. Each Christmas morning, they would go to Rasmus' grave and place a wreath. This continued year after year until one day, after living a very long and productive life, Laurel too was gathered to her Christ and all the saints. Stepping across the finishing line of this life into the next, Laurel was greeted by the Christ and received the "laurel crown of victory" about which the Apostle Paul boasted. There beside Jesus was Rasmus waiting to greet his fine wife. Beaming with delight, the two fell into a hearty embrace that they will enjoy for an eternity.

About the Author

R obert Cameron Malcolm IV is a 1977 graduate of Westminster College, New Wilmington, PA, with a Master of Divinity Degree from Pittsburgh Theological Seminary in 1981. He served Natrona Heights Presbyterian Church for 30 years as their pastor and youth group leader after pastoring and leading the youth ministry at the First Presbyterian Church of Bentleyville, PA. In 2018, he produced his first book, *A History of the Natrona Heights Presbyterian Church*. In 2020, his second book, *Mary Magdalene: New Testament Eve* was published.

WA